Roam

Roaming Revelator

A disillusioned soul running from his past and scared of his future, but more fearful of his own mind!

Book 1 of the Revelator Trilogy

Mark Huck

YouCaxton Publications

Oxford & Shrewsbury

Dedicated to all those who have supported me; I could not have done it without you. Equally, thanks to those that didn't believe in me - you made me work harder to achieve.

Contents

CHAPTER 1:

CHASING A LIFE

The road is wild; the road is calm, the road is your friend, the road is your enemy…the road is everything!

Standing here, a 'wild man of the world' contemplating the road of life, avoiding the norms and herds of people, long greying hair falling on to a face covered by the lines of life and an unkempt long beard, in a scruffy tight pair of jeans and an old leather jacket, with no place to go and no place to be, looking over the road that is weaving towards distant towns. The question spins around in his mind;

"Am I free or am I trapped? Who would even know?"

Questioning the road his life has taken to this point;

"Am I successful? What is success? What did I want? What do I want?"

Standing here in scuffed boots, with weathered clothes many would suggest not, but his swirling mind starts again;

"I am more successful than I could have imagined? Yet not successful! Who judges success? Who judges what makes a life?"

Reflecting and finding these inner revelations of himself, hindsight is a wonderful thing; but foresight would be better to avoid the problem in the first place. If only Dan had this foresight and had learned from his mistakes, how different would his life have been? Would it have been better? Or could it have been worse? He knew that one thing is true; foresight may have helped him avoid the problems his winding road has led to. Would foresight have meant avoiding the need to run? Avoiding the need to be fleeing with blood on his hands, after losing his temper? With foresight would he have ended up beating a man half to death?

His torturous mind continuing to torment him;

"What does it prove anyway? am I a 'bigger man'? am I 'hard man'? am I a hero or a violent psychopath? When I shed the blood who am I? Would I choose differently changing my revelations and my hindsight into foresight? "

Dan's emotions are continuously mixing like the air and fuel of his bike, and creating a just as explosive reaction, forcing his pistons up and down, the demons keep him grounded, but fuel an ever mixed up response, questioning what is right and what is wrong? The mixed good and bad in his crazy mind continuing to do battle;

"Who actually dictates what is right from wrong? Should I have learned from the first time I spilled blood, or actually does blood need to be spilled? Do you need to defend like a Viking? Is honour and revenge a necessary evil of life?"

Dan had lived life at full throttle so when challenged his reaction is like the 0-60 of his power crazed bike, thumping away till he runs out of fuel, his tank is big and the fuel always full, creating a dangerous reaction at every twist of his life.

Back in his current reality, Dan slowly contemplates looking for his own revelations on life, deep in the heart, success rages like a bull and failure weighs like a lead weight in equal measure, defining the polar opposite rise and fall from happiness to sorrow and rebirthing of happiness, a never ending cycle happening faster than he can finish this rapidly cooling cup of coffee. The sweet smell of the fields basking in the sun evokes a feeling of content, but that feeling is crushed by the urges to discover, to be, to move forward, forever moving never staying too long. Having worked and lived in the same place for 30 years, to then be tossed on the scrap heap redundant, is enough to give you the desire never to stay long anywhere, there is time for that in when you lay in the wooden box.

The mindless questions surrounding this feeling are far deeper and harder to define; "however I do know I search for success and happiness, with every passing moment the chase for this stretches surrounding the success with it, forever rolling in front of me, a ball rolling down a hill faster than I can give chase, but chase I do and hard I chase."

All he knew is that it's once again time to hit the open road and set himself free and start again, forever wind in the face come rain or shine. Flowing into the weaving road towards the distant times, once again whole, invisible to the herds as he roared off along the road, leaving behind the single empty coffee cup on the table, like a once hopeful dream used and discarded as the dust from the departure settles the cup is empty like the dream it once held.

Riding into town the light is fading and the streets are quiet, Dan parks his old motorbike outside a 'run down' hotel, the town is small with only a church on the distant hill and a few small businesses on the road. An eerie silence hangs in the air, coupled with a greasy smell from the only place that looks open, a small hotel with grubby curtains and a half lit sign saying 'Vacancies'. He'd stayed in worse and enjoyed it he thought.

Dan checked into the hotel and headed straight for the room, trying to dodge the disapproving looks from the; dressed to impress cheap suited types at the bar, who sneer and look down their noses as he struts past dirty and tired, in his scruffy *"don't care if I impress type clothes"* He only wanted to impress the people who matter in life, not the no name judgement brigade. Today nobody mattered, so impress who? Nobody that's who! not even himself. The cheap suited lot, stop and stare like a pack of wolves eyeing up prey, looking down their all too perfect noses as they turn their backs deeming him unnecessary, the noise once again escalates and Dan strides off into the lift.

As he stares into the mirror in the dimly lit small room the inner torments begin again;

"Am I free? What is freedom? What have I become? Who actually am I? What do I want?"

The room does not answer for the road is the teacher. The room is cold and damp, with no tea or coffee, no mini bar, the window is slightly ajar and the gentle wind whistles slightly through it. The reality is dark and dank coupled with retro furniture, developing a mix of old and mould.

What he actually wants is a hazy escape from reality, opening the bottle of Whiskey he had in his small duffel bag, the smell hits him and instantly gives him a smile of gratification, knowing the next few sips were going to be sharp but take him on a journey, where nobody knows his name not even himself.

As the bottle started to empty, Dan slumped in the chair in the corner of his room, just in a pair of jeans, the top three buttons undone and his tee shirt flung on the bed. His once clear head, full of hopes and dreams, slowly becomes emptier. The darkness of his mind becomes quiet, the race and urgency in his soul slows. This dank room smelt like it hadn't been used for years, the wall paper is peeling and yellowing, the white tiles had chips and cracks with dirt stuck in them. Only one thing to do, sip from the sharp teat of escapism......draw in that mind numbing liquid that saps imagination bringing with it a sense of calm, nuzzled into the bosom of his old comforting friend, slowly he drifts into the nothingness of his haze, still slumped in the chair.

The next morning comes all too quickly, with all the aches and pains gained by a life lived to the fullest and a night in a chair. Dan stands in his pants with a cigarette and a half drunk bottle of Whiskey, the onslaught of his questioning mind attack him again;

"Am I too old for this? What else could I be doing?"

With a draw of his cigarette and swig of Whiskey he heads for the shower. No fancy soap, just a cheap bottle of something left by the maid, emptying the contents into his large hand stained with oil from his bike, rubbing the liquid all over himself, there is moment of joy and warmth, a soul rebirthing and a feeling of something, something is better than nothing. As he rubs the liquid soap all over himself, there is moment of joy and warmth with a soul rebirthing and feeling something, something is better than nothing. Sometimes you have to hurt to really feel.

Standing in the bathroom dripping on the floor feeling the aches and pains return, looking in his wallet with only a few notes left and not much more in the bank, he stood naked and now creating a puddle on the white tilled floor, it's time for the old '*run for the hills*'

technique he has used since he was a teenager, check in for 3 nights then do a 'runner' after the first night. By the time they notice he will be long gone from this dirt infested two horse town to who knows where? Off on the road again roaring away from the hotel on a bike loud enough to wake the dead.

The feeling of guilt fell heavy in Dan's stomach, leaving without paying was getting harder as he got older but still a necessary evil on the road of life.....the redundancy money was not going to get him much further, neither is the bike which has needed fuel for the last few miles.

As Dan pulled into get fuel he was amused by the slightly too old for that skirt length, waitress serving inside. As he pumped the fuel a familiar smell of the golden nectar feeding life into the beating heart of his machine, filling himself once again with hopes and dreams. Dan couldn't help but stare at this woman. Cheapened and scared by the drudgery of her life, the stress and torture of her days written on her face like lines in a book, his thoughts rampage around his mind;

"Has she got a husband? Does she care? Does he make her happy? Does he make her knees still go weak when he makes love to her? Or is he wham bam thank u mam where's my dinner type?"

As he walked into pay for the fuel he passed a young guy with a look of entitlement, a look of ownership, a smugness only a silver spoon generation could possess, Dan stared straight at him with his best Clint Eastwood look, the young guy was already staring at him, eyeing him up with a look of disgust as he picks up his phone and takes a picture of his salad, the dark side of Dan's mind starts to raise its ugly head;

"How far could I shove that phone down his throat?"

The thought left him cold and sick to in his stomach, but with a dislike for the now self-obsessed, selfish generation that has no idea of humanity, Dan's thought turned darker than the paintwork on his bike;

"I would love to kick him all over this place and watch him bleed into his Keen Wha salad".

Dan paid for his fuel and the two day hunger started to bite at him again, but the money left was tight. A man has to eat but not this salad shit the pussy boy with the phone is nibbling on, so he can keep his feminine look with his saggy skinny jeans. The smell of the restaurant was greasy with a smell of old fat hanging in the air and more akin with Dan's old school diet, the place looks old school like it had stood still for decades. Old brown and yellow wallpaper with a chrome serving hatch, has this place been made to look 1970's or is it still in the 1970's?

'Food I have to eat'

The thought spirals around his head fighting with his other desires that rampage around his endocrine system, but I need more than that; I have desires, so strong I could turn myself inside out trying to quench my lust and need for thrill, I am not sure anymore what satisfies me the most, sex or danger or dangerous sex but what I do know is, I need to feel my heat beat hard, to know I am still alive. Without the gratification of a pounding heart and sweat running down hid back he might as well be dead, as he felt nothing till his heart was above 3 figures anyway.

"But food I need real food, greasy bacon with a runny egg and enough tea to drown my desires in"

Sitting on the smooth cold leather bench seat with the well-worn mahogany table was an ash tray 'why would there be an ashtray? It had been decades since anyone could smoke in a public place, maybe this place is actually 20 years behind' the slightly too old for the short tight dress waitress is now walking towards him; 'wow she is sexy' she was about 35, no ring with bitten nails and hair that is as black as the night itself, 'I bet she has never bought a drink any night of the week' As she walked over she looked at Dan, her stride changed crossing her feet as she walks, smiling in way that makes my heart approach 3 figures 'what is it about her? Why does she intrigue me?' then she opened her mouth leant forward allowing her uniform to flop down so he could see the black and white bra she was wearing his heart smashed 3 figures and his blood ran as cold as ice but raged with the intensity of a towering inferno.

"What can I get you?"

Dan's chaotic rushing mind spills around in his head 'Well fuck me! That answer can go 2 ways, I can already feel my blood pounding in my veins, hammering around my body, what can she get me? Naked, high or both would be a start' but as he gathered his thoughts and deepened his voice.

"Black coffee, all day breakfast and whatever else u can give me!"

Smiling, he rolled his head back and gave her the look he gave through all his life to get what he wanted from women, maybe having slightly less impact than 20 years ago, but she still gave him back a twinkle in her eyes, she replied;

*"So you want coffee, breakfast and whatever you can get.......
maybe you will get what you want!"*

She winked and strutted off back to the till; she looked over her shoulder and pushed her pen between her ruby red lips. Dan's body was shaking with desire, but sex would not be enough today, it would calm his beating desires and set him up for the day, but today he needed more! He needed to live like today is the last day. Today was going to be one of those days, a wild day, a dangerous day, maybe this was the day he'd find himself again, maybe it will be the day he loses himself forever.

He wasn't even sure he knew who, or what, he was looking for anymore. As Dan watched her on her tiptoe reaching to put fresh coffee beans in the machine her legs extend and so did his pulse, that tight red uniform with white edging details could just, she turned and caught his stare, he was practically drooling she looked embarrassed yet confident, the irresistible mix he craved.

Phone boy was walking over is his linen trousers rolled up with no socks and what looked like slippers, he reminded Dan of the old fashioned knitted jumper placed over the shoulders, yuppie type from the 1980's, surely he would not come over to him. He still wanted to ram his phone anywhere he could push it, he gave Dan that smile that says, I am so much better than you 'fuck I am going to lose my shit over him, 20 years ago I would have thrown him over the table by now and educated him on his personality deficit, with multiple education being repeated into his head'

The waitress looked over at Dan with a smile which changed his whole demeanour, with a look of enticement and wonderment. Her poker straight hair was loosely tied up, as she moved her hair fell gently to the side exposing her slender neckline, accentuating her high cheek bones and her perfect sleek jaw line. While the cerebral battle rampaged in his mind, the age old battle of man occurred, the questions pushing Dan further than he can handle;

"Why am I here what am doing? Woman or war. This skinny, tall, goofy, twenty-something kid pushing my primordial rage to war, but this curvy pear shaped, short skirted waitress equally raises a primordial desire?"

All this without any coffee or breakfast yet, the pit of his stomach burned with an unhealthy swirl between rage and lust.

The phone boy swaggered up;

"How much?"

Looking at his phone before she even had chance to reply 'the youth are so fucking rude' as the youth held out his phone and swipes the machine, without even acknowledging the waitress at all, starting a video chat conversation on his phone;

"You would not believe this place it's such a shit hole, not even got a vegan menu, hey, look at this!" He spun the phone round to face the waitress *"This must be what happens when pretty but stupid girls can't cut it as strippers"*

'What the fuck!' The goofy little prick was laughing in that fake, not funny but I want to be loud and obnoxious kind of way. Before this thought had risen fully through his mind, Dan's pulse was so far in excess of three figures he could feel his heart beating hard in his chest, trying to smash its way through the rib cage with the force of a sledgehammer, the taste and smell of blood already filling his mouth and nose, he had bitten so hard trying to control himself, he'd bitten through part of his bottom lip, With the blood slowly seeping south of his lips he screamed;

"You mother fucking ignorant prick"

Leaping over the table and on to the next, splattering a left over breakfast across the floor, the plate smashed sending tomato juice splashing up the brown wallpaper, the noise of the plate smashing was still ringing around the restaurant, with everyone silently stunned and staring as he landed in front of him, his face distorted, confused and his floppy hair already flopping over his face, he was taller than Dan and much younger but only half Dan's weight, as he grabbed his throat with his left hand and smashed the right into his face repeatedly, he went limp in Dan's hands, as Dan let him fall to the floor it gave him a really short burst of a high, leaving his head spinning like a cocaine fuelled orgasm.

He'd not felt like this in a while, but the rage was coming back just as he lifted his boot to stamp on his semi-conscious face, the waitress pushed her slim arm into his chest, as Dan looked at her with a mix of rage and excitement she smiled and kicked her flat shoe straight into the arrogant youth's groin, he doubled over with the look of a dying wasp. He was lucky! Dan's blow to his face was going to be much more devastating! She looked Dan in the eye with a mix and excitement covering her face and said;

"Get me out of here!"

As he began to slow his racing mind and take back the control of his rage, repressing the desire to continue educating the lifeless youth who is clutching his groin as he lay on the floor. Dan looked around at the shear horror on the faces of the innocent herds of people who had witness this atrocity, the tormenting thought returned.

"Was it his fault? Did the little shit deserve it, should he have stayed in his seat?"

They rushed out the double doors flinging them wide making them clang and rattle against the walls of the building. He led her to the bike, a black behemoth of a bike, a love affair that only the road understands. The largest motorbike engine ever made. This big black beast had seen more action than this waitress. Dan saw the unsure look in her face, throwing his leg over the bike;

"I am leaving, stay or leave!"

He pressed the starter button the wild engine roared into life and they left in a frenzy of noise dust and turmoil. With the ruckus behind them and the sun beating down, he felt alive, he felt the beating of his heart and the rushing of blood, he could hear it, feel it and literally taste it, he could feel how much his lip hurt as the dirt and grit bounced off of it, at least he felt it, at least he felt alive, he felt free!

As he rode he could feel Joanne (he guessed that was her name from her uniform badge) gripping him tighter and tighter, they needed distance between there and them, but wow did he feel alive, the feeling of being alive normally cost him, once his freedom too, the road was his savior, his teacher and his life. Approaching three figures on the bike, Joanne was really gripping her hands tighter and tighter into his sides, gripping the old supple leather of the jacket, the haze of the moment made a confused mess spinning in his head, the smell of fuel and grease still hanging in his nose, the road was leading and he was but a follower.

The road was winding and quiet with no place to stop, a seamless ribbon of delight and curiosity, giving him his medicine to calm, delight, to satisfy. They needed a sanctuary, a place to be, a place to allow some calm back into their world. The old church loomed on the hill 'point and shoot that's the place to gather our thoughts and find out what to do with Joanne'

Walking into the quiet church, with the bike parked behind some bushes, the silence and space was almost repressive, the smell of damp in the air and the dirt on the windows made it look like a horror movie location, with an overgrown garden and creaky doors to boot. Each step produced a melancholy feeling; the wooden floor was well worn and slippery with a thin moss. The light was shining through a high up window and producing a shaft of light to a small doorway at the back of the alter, the ornate hinges were covered in rust and cobwebs, Joanne looked terrified, her eyes were wide and her hair was matted the wind in her hair had seen to that, no longer straight, the wild wind from the helmet less blast down the black and white ribbon of road, which had tangled her once pristine hair. Messy hair gave her the bad girl look and that black and white ribbon of road kept the thought of her black and white bra firmly in the forefront of his tangled mind which again began to ask;

"Why do you want her, what was it, why can you not concentrate on anything but her?"

Joanne was standing with her head down and her medium sized breasts stretching the material around the press studs on her uniform as she asked;

"Do you think I went too far?"

"No but you did stop me from going too far, but what now? Do you have any place to be?"

The words echoed around as if asking the question and repeating the words over and over, they hung so long in the air as if there could be no answer.

Her silence answered the question but her face told a different story, one of sorrow and regret, she answered quietly;

"No. Not anymore! Just a place I put some stuff once, it's not important".

Sensing a troubled heavy heart and a story he was not sure he wanted to hear.

"So, where do we go from here? I brought you and put you in danger, but what next? Do I leave you or drop you off somewhere? What do you want?"

"What do I want? That is a question I have never answered. Well I need food, drink and many other things, I need to keep moving on. Oh I forgot 'Mr what else I can get, do you always get it'?"

Dan shifted awkwardly looking up at the shaft of light and with a long pause he grunted;

"I used to."

Joanne looked at him with a look of curiosity and a slightly pensive turn of her head;

"I know nothing of you not even your name and you know nothing of me apart from my name, we are trapped in this moment, a moment that feels like it could last a lifetime, but as ever will end up hurting, everything does!"

Dan turned and lowered his gaze, she could see the light illuminating him like a scruffy angel, with the shaft of light shining so bright behind him, his stern steely exacting eyes, stared straight into her, giving her a mixed feeling of dread and excitement. He was not the best looking man to ever stand before her, but the strength in his eyes weakened her, his voice broke the silence;

"What do you want?"

"Fun! I am sick of my humdrum life working all hours for just enough food to eat! But what do you want?"

He looked her up and down, then with a slightly softer yet still stern voice;

"Right now I want to step over to you grab your hair, pull your head back so I can kiss your neck, biting your ear lobe and lifting

that short uniform up to grab that bum.......what do I want? I want to take you and excite every part of your body making your toes curl as you orgasm over and over till you beg me to stop, that's actually what I want! "

She paused and looked at the floor, biting her bottom ruby red lip as she looked up at him and in her cheeky provocative voice;

"Well, maybe you will get what you want".

He strode with confidence like the king of the jungle, thrusting his hands into the hair on the sides of her head, the cuff of his leather jacket brushing over her ears and his fingers caught in her tangled hair, the two lock lips and she kissed him as hard as he kissed her, he worked his way across her face, he pulled her hair with one hand and with his other hand grasped a full handful of her bum, digging his nails in through the red uniform, just as he prepared to bite her ear she shook in his hands, quivering from her head to her toes, Dan lifted her up by her waist as she wrapped her long slender legs around his body as he ran his hands through his hair while she kissed him.

Sliding her red uniform up revealing a perfect round bum for him to hold on too, he moved over to the large wooden table next to the alter, adorned with silver candle holders and a green table runner embroiled in gold, he laid her gently down on her back, his look matched hers, a look of lust, a look of passion; smelling her excitement, dying to see that uniform expose her curves and that black and white bra that has resided in his mind since she took his order. He grabbed the front of her uniform, he ripped open the press studs to reveal everything he wanted right now, her black and white bra gripping her pert breasts and with her waistline moving out to her full hips. The heat ran straight up his back into his head, throwing his jacket off and almost ripping his shirt off to reveal a body better than many men half his age, no abs but chiselled non the less.

He lunged his face between her breasts pulling her hair in a way that excited her more, he moved his head down biting and kissing across her stomach to her hips, with a pause he then buried his head between her thighs pulling her on to his face, digging his fingers into her hips, her hands pushing his head harder on to her pussy, he felt how wet her pants were on his face, he pulled them to one side and she writhed in ecstasy unable to even scream, as he showed his experience of life, licking sucking and blowing on to her clit, he plunged two fingers inside her straight on to her G spot and her back arched as she buried her hands into his hair, she let out an unearthly scream and dug her fingers into the back of his head.

She rolled and bucked on the table knocking off the silver candelabra's, which sensationally smashed south, crashing into the floor tiles and echoing around the grey stone walls, enhancing the moment like a big orchestra band with crashing symbols heightening her pleasure, with her knees high around his head she violently rolled from side to side, rocking his head as if trying to snap it off with the motion, till she could take no more and pushed his head away. She was left panting and lay exposed on the table every inch of her body pulsating, her toes curled her hands holding on to the edges of the tables, with a single bead of sweat nestled in between her breasts. Dan wiped his mouth with the side of his hand, smiling reliving the taste and smell of this woman, a scent that draws him in like a prowling cat elegantly moving closer slowly and surely, the shaft of light from the stained glass window making his body glisten with a post orgasmic sweat, he stood with his large well defined muscular chest dominating her view from the table.

She looked at him with all the happiness of a young virgin but the slutty-ness of a whore, her hair messy but sexy, she leaned forward and kissed him, she could taste herself on his lips. She rolled over lifting her bum in the air and said;

"Take me"

Her bum so round and big, she arched her back and thrust it upwards, making it a gift to him, Dan's heart rate went off the scale as he moved in closer, his rock hard cock pulled the top of his jeans away from his stomach;

"Make me come again"

Dan dropped his jeans and the big metal buckle clattered to the floor echoing around the church, he climbed on top of her and slowly thrust deep inside her, her mind-bending feeling consumed her as the tip pushed inside her till it was pushing her G spot against the cold table, she felt him pushing against her with his balls bagging against her clit, his fingers dug into her hips, as he pushed against the table it was even more intense, the cold wood heightening her senses and the old wooden table making everything magnified, the table runner half under her right breast dangling towards the floor, as he thrusted and thrusted harder and harder his sweat was running down between his strong shoulders, she loved him grabbing her hair squeezing her bum, leaving red marks where he had been, how as he got so many hands? They were everywhere, dragging his nails down her back, spanking her bum, teasing her with faster, then slower, motions some deep, some shallow, she was on the verge of another orgasm when he grabbed her hair, she screamed like a banshee as she came, he let out a noise like an animal protecting his herd, animalistic and dominant. Collapsing on to the table tangled in a lovers' embrace both hearts beating as one single heart. The moment felt perfect as if time had stopped for them.

As he lay there with his arms around her waist, her curvy bum nuzzled into his groin she felt protected and satisfied like no other man had managed before, her clitoris tingling, her heart beating hard and her skin electrified, he lay there in equal glory in a euphoric haze with his cock still inside her, his heart beating so hard she could feel it against her back, he had fucked her body but made love to her mind, she had been drawn to him from the moment he walked into her life as a protector, a giver, a leading light of manliness, his confidence and ability to convey his attitude of 'no fucks' will be given today over anybody. He was her fun and her escapism, her road to something else, the freedom and new beginnings, he had awoken something she had not felt in a long time, hope and desire.

"We need to think what next, this as beautiful as it is won't keep us moving"

Joanne looked puzzled;

"Where do we need to move to?"

"This is only temporary we don't know how long this place will be safe"

"Let's at least look around."

She muttered slightly annoyed her moment of pleasure was now being cut short;

"I don't even know your name"

"Names what are names? Does it make a difference? Matthew, Mark Luke or John what does it matter!"

"It matters I want to know, I actually want to go where you're going; I have no place to be so, no plans just a road and you! Let's just see where we go, but I would like to at least know your name"

"Dan my name is Dan"

Pulling his jeans up over his semi erect penis that filled his white pants, the sight of it stretching the tight white material, which gave her one last mini shudder of joy.

CHAPTER 2:

RUNNING FOR A LIFE

A s their eyes scouted around the dusty old church, the well-worn mahogany benches still had cushions on them. The place felt deserted yet used, candles were still burning down in their holders, footprints visible in the dirt towards the back of the church, some rubbish on the floor, wrappers of some kind and plastic bags

"Joanne this place is really strange, deserted yet lived in, I can't see who would come here it's not been used as a church for many years, the stained glass was cracked and dirty and looked like trees were blocking the light to most of the windows"

The silence was broken by a loud creaking that made Joanne jump and her already tingling skin run cold. Dan had opened the small ornate door at the back of the church and was looking inside. Lifting the light switch outside the door, a dim light inside flickered into life. As Dan stepped inside and disappeared inside the corridor, the smell of moss and natural decay hit his nostrils, he thought to himself that nobody has cared for this place in a long time; the paint was flaking too with yellow water marks that created patterns on the faded and grubby flaking paintwork. A couple of doors, one each side of corridor were ajar.

Moving closer to the doors, the hairs on Dan's neck pricked, his flesh goose pimpled and his nerves on edge, the blood in his body rampaged through his veins, his fight or flight instinct battling with him, curiosity and intrigue dragged him towards to the doors. He was stood between both doors with all of his testosterone flooding into his body, urging him to stride through one of the doors, but his instinct for self-preservation adding thoughts into his mind from every horror movie he had ever seen.

Slowly opening the door on his right, no creaks just silence, this was clearly a well-used door as he slowly pushed it open he saw the wet oil on the hinges, his engineering mind drew him to analyse everything. His fear and tantalising curiosity pulled him towards the room, his desire to know what was in the room forced him through the door. The light switch was old and the light fitting loose on the wall but it illuminated the room. The room is neat with an old expensive a well-used table at one end of the room, with folders and other stationary neatly placed on it, the walls smarter, not fresh but having been decorated more recently. Laid on the floor are some flattened plastic bags, large rectangular and black, rolls of tape next to them and a slightly sweet incense smell in the air like something had been burned to cover a smell. He moved over to the table which had locked drawers on either side of the table, he tried each one of them; they rattled but remained secure in their position.

Looking around the room Dan noticed some black overalls which were hung behind the door, with masks hung on the pegs too, a single baseball bat in the corner, no glove or ball to be seen. Suddenly Dan's fear reached its peak, his stomach knotted and sickness consuming his brain. The questioning from within his soul began once again;

"What the fuck do people need black overalls and masks for? This is no trick or treat outfit!"

Laid next to the overalls was an ornate wooden chest, clean but very old, gold decorative straps surrounding it. Encasing it was a single hasp with a modern padlock hanging from it. His mind asked him;

"Why would someone put such a big lock on this box?"

Particularly as the hasp is made of gold and easily broken. The pins securing the folding part of the hasp were worn with the securing ends very thin.

"What is this place? What is in this box?"

Taking his multi tool out of his jacket pocket, he unfolded the pliers and screwdrivers in the handle, they folded out like a Swiss army knife, he grabbed the hinge pin on the hasp and started to wiggle it and pull at it, although it moved he couldn't pull it through, he whacked the pliers against the pin like a hammer, the noise echoing down the corridor till it reached Joanne who was sat on one of the pews rummaging through her small purse. Dan, like a man possessed consumed by finishing what he started, fighting back the fear and the sickness, replaced with hard-headed bloody mindedness to open the chest.

Joanne wasn't sure what the noise was, but feeling safe as her protector was down that corridor, she strutted playfully down the corridor imagining what delights she might take from Dan this time, her sense awoken her desire full and her body needing more than her mind could comprehend, her mind swirled high and her soul bright, causing her to skip along the corridor with no fear at all the just the delight of life running through her veins.

He yanked at the pin that he had bashed most of the way through the hinge, Dan was completely consumed by the task, his forehead red his temple veins bulging and his desire to open the chest stronger than his fear, sweat forming on his brow and running cold down the side of his head, oblivious to all around him, just a single focus and the determination to succeed consuming him, with a final yank the pin flew out of the hinge, which sent Dan rolling on to his back, the pain of the fall on to his back, contorted his face and brought with it a feeling of discontent, dazed and slightly confused, with a feeling slightly light headed haze in his head.

Almost skipping into the room Joanne laughs;

"What are you doing? Have I worn you out?"

Pulling himself to his feet Dan muttered;

"Wear me out? You would be lucky...."

He leans forward and opened the box. A wave of delight flooded through his body his eyes wide and his mouth wider still, the velvet interior containing bags of white powder next to neatly stacked and bound notes, thousands of pounds with a rolled up cloth placed on top of the money, extending over the full length of the chest; they both let out a gasp in unison, a shared moment of shock, excitement and hope, as he unrolled the old cloth it revealed a picture of a red God with 3 faces and 3 eyes in each face and skulls around the faces, with the amount he knows about art, his initial thought is; Some odd fancy art bull shit clearly, what would anyone want with this ugly looking picture?

As he looked up at Joanne his face spoke before his lips could move, an expression of horror spread across his face.

"This is far more dangerous than we should be mixed up in! I brought you here but now we have to leave, this is not a place to be, quaint as it maybe it's a debauchery of danger more than we should be part of!"

"Hold on there "Mr whatever else I can get" this is just starting to be fun let's take it, let's live a little, let's get fucked, blued and tattooed, let's live!"

Crashing through the door a tall well-built man boomed;

"Who the fuck are you?"

Stood in the doorway he filled it, his bald head had a tattoo of a snake around one ear onto his temple, the tattoo glared at them with as much evil as the Neanderthal who just crashed in.

Joanne let out a scream louder than when Dan had his head between her legs that felt as if it shook the whole building.

Dan jumped to his feet with the cash spilling from his hands.....the Neanderthal deepened he voice and repeated;

"Who the fuck are you?"

This time the words cut through Dan with the feeling of a Japanese war sword, Dan's mind was in a ferocious panic fighting with fight or talk. This man was three times his size filling the only door in the room, Dan's options were limited, fight dirty or talk,

"If he gets one good move on me I am a dead man........ I will be lying in a cold   stone room with nobody even aware of where I am"

Purposefully perplexed and simply stuttering to make the Neanderthal think, trying to pretend he was a no body who stumbled across this by accident, Dan frantically started talking;

"We, we, we just stopped to have sex in the church......my fantasy not hers we were just exploring I ddddidn't mean to find this or cause any trouble"

The Neanderthal cut deeper with a harsher voice, like a sergeant major with a virgin platoon;

"BULL SHIT, look at you and your woman who do you work for? Who sent you?"

"Nnnnnnooooo bbbooody it's the truth I didn't mean too"

As the Neanderthal stepped forward he raised his fists to make him look even more menacing. Suddenly he let out an almighty moan, as Joanne hit him in the face with an ornate gold staff, dropping him to his knees, he screamed in agony, the blood glistened on the staff with two serpents heads one now covered in blood.

Joanne was frozen to the spot looking as if she has seen Lucifer himself. As the Neanderthal started to stand Dan kicked him square in the face with his steel toecap boot, the noise of cracking bone rupturing the air as he fell onto his back, the blood running from his face, the snake on his temple already covered in blood from Joanne's blow;

"Shit or bust now darlin.....We are fucked if he talks to anybody, the best way now is a silent witness"

With that, Dan grabbed the staff raised it above his head and with the demented look of a man who was summoning up all the pain a world could offer, he gritted his teeth and emitted a battle cry of terror, as he drove the serpent staff straight into the Neanderthal's face over and over, Dan's heart body and soul intoxicated with adrenaline, anger and his past torture's all flooding to the forefront of his mind, the staff so far into this now concave bloody mess of a face, Dan could no longer pull it out, the staff wedged in to the bone standing proud all on its own, this was not a moment to be proud, not a moment to stand basking in his triumph, this was a return to his darker days, the days when he could not control his anger.

He stood back and was breathing heavy, his chest seemingly taking in barrels of oxygen, he turned his head slightly towards Joanne fearing this is the last time he would see her. Who would want to spend time with such a deranged beast of such ferocity? If only she knew he had killed to protect her and stop this snake from hurting her.

From the corner of Dan's eye, he sees a face of wonderment, a face of pleasure and excitement. Joanne looked at him and smiled;

"That was so mother fucking intense"

Joanne's voice loud and squeaky,

"Is he dead?"

"Well he won't be talking. Are you sure you're okay? That was not how I intended our first day together to end up?"

Joanne was pacing back and forth with her uniform hanging half off her shoulder, with that black and white bra exposed;

"He's fucking dead you fucking killed him"

Her voice still squeaking;

"Wow what a buzz I feel high as a kite I have never seen a dead body."

"Joanne, killing a man is no delight, killing a man is no pleasure and definitely not a high to be savoured!"

Dan's voice was sombre deep and precise, gone was the three figure heart and heavy breathing replaced by the smell of blood with a sicking feeling of guilt and sorrow. This was always the feeling Dan had when went too far and he knew what was to come next, the pain in his head from the stress, caused by the guilt, the remorse, the sorrow, the need to justify the action. The only salvation he has ever had, himself!

The thoughts and questions were already raging around Dan's mind;

"We are what are we do? Why is it we do? Can a wrong be erased? Can a crime against humanity be forgiven? Or am I doomed to roam carrying the regret of all those I have hurt, wearing my crown of thorns upon my head and the stains of pain on my soul?"

Dan broke the silence;

"Let's leave now Joanne, we need the money grab as much as you can carry, bring that rolled up cloth too so I can clean myself up"

Gathering up all the money stuffing into every pocket and pushing it inside the well-aged leather jacket, they stepped over the corpse lay on the floor with a gold staff buried deep into its head, the blood pooling on the floor and turning a darker shade of red as it started to dry. He took her hand;

"Watch your step beautiful"

The words stopped her racing heart with a flutter, a smile slowly crept over her face and her eyes filled with emotion. 'Beautiful' it had been a long time since she had been called that by a man.

The church felt darker, quieter and definitely colder, every step echoed and they headed along the aisle the smell is stronger, how could this place feel now so repulsive? The flag stones beneath Dan's feet shifted as he masterfully strode out as if on parade. The one shaft of light was highlighting the dust in the air, Joanne's posture matching Dan's, replicating his arrogance and strength, little did she know how he wanted to curl up and die.;

"It never gets any easier killing a man"

He muttered as he passed row after row of well-worn pews. His soul felt like it was being dragged down into a darky sticky swamp.

Joanne face was the polar opposite, excited like a child and her church felt bright like a spring day, her steps bouncy and light, with the feeling of joy creeping into her heart, she started to enjoy the feeling of power, intoxicated completely by the feeling it had given her, she had found her leading light who can do no wrong, who enticed and thrilled her.

Leaving the old wooden door of the church the bright sunshine briefly blinded both of them, covering their eyes with their hands, they ran for the bush the bike was parked behind scurrying as if escaping a fire, a smile drew across Dan's face as he saw his black shiny saviour, his sanctuary waiting for him, his rescue and his lifeline all bundled up in a black and chrome package. Dan stuffed the money and cloth in his duffle bag and pulled out an old spare open face helmet and goggles, glimpsing over at Joanne, he watched her straightening up her uniform, hiding her black with white ribbon bra, Dan's heart rate increased, the hair on his arms and neck all standing up as the blood around his brain rushes to his flaccid penis, engorging it and making his jeans tight. Dan's desires were insatiable, with the easy trigger of a teenage boy, a glimpse of a bra and he was ready to go again, to take her on any fantasy she desired in a hedonistic flurry of orgasmic explosion. He looked at her with lust, the wrinkles around his eyes dominant but all telling, a man of experience, a man of the world, unfortunately an old world that was slowly decaying around him; the world he once shared, not as he remembers it but an awful representation of the utopia he had dreamed of as a boy. Now all he cared about is making his utopia for his life, *'You get what you give'* used to be his mantra, now he was older it was more *'You get what you create!'* Everything was because of a choice you made; even things that were not caused by you are set by your reaction to the situation. A set of thoughts that had shaped his very *'raison d'être'*.

The twinkle in Joanne's eyes sparked a feeling Dan is not familiar with, a feeling that crept up his spine and melted the intensity that rampaged around his head, 'what was it?' Whatever it is it's a feeling he barley remembered and tossed aside with ease. As he saddled up on the black beast, his newly awoken princess needed no encouragement to take the open face helmet and jump on behind him, sinking into to the soft leather saddle and gripping her black knight tightly;

"Hold the fuck on this is going to be a bumpy ride."

With that he ripped the throttle back, spinning the rear wheel, which bucked violently sideways to the right like a stallion being broken for the first time, struggling for grip and showering stones behind them, kicking up dust, he wrestled with the bike, keeping it upright as he leaned the bike over to the right the wheels kicks out to the left creating a dust cloud as if trying to hide them from view, Dan's peacock display of confidence was typical of him when he was around a woman, never was he the type to be flustered or embarrassed, just a show of a tail feather that he loved to display to anyone that would look.

Leaving the car park, the wheel picks up the black and white ribbon of road sending the front wheel up in the air, a slight dab of rear brake bringing it down gracefully (never underestimate an old grey man Dan thought to himself) tearing down the tree lined road, the trees stood as soldiers lining up on parade, the wind in his face only shielded by his sunglasses. It's the old run for the hills again; looking skyward Dan knew this skyline as he is entering the county of his youth, the fatherland with its wild landscape, twisty roads, danger on every corner and plenty of places to lose yourself, so run for the hills, run for home. He pulled back the throttle slowly, the bike was both master and apprentice on the roadof life, the torque beneath their legs vibrated and growled, sending a wave of happiness through Dan but an entirely different shock of happiness through Joanne. As the vibrations intensify so did her still pulsing pussy, this bike seemed to have its own language, communicating on a level that vibrated her entire pelvis, taking her from mildly excited to horny as hell.

Each gear change created a pop and vibration from the engine which shook her from below the waist too deep into her mind. A tingling spine, a pulsing wet patch in her pants and a constant state of mild arousal, this could be a long ride! Slinking back against the backrest she slipped into a heady state of euphoria and let it happen, just enjoying the ride.

On the back of the bike she felt safe, she felt secure, her fingers still sore from holding on to the soft old leather jacket, after Dan had kicked the bike around in the gravel car park and looked after all three of them, safe she definitely felt! Hanging on to Dan, with only her new found trust that this man will protect her, against absolutely anything that could come their way. A feeling of warmth flooded from her stomach up her spine and reduced the adrenaline fuelled cocktail she was experiencing, slowing her mind down, replacing it with a content feeling, a wild man slightly aged with a soft caring but brutal danger to him, could he be the bad boy with the softer side? The rarest of all men, a bad boy who cares?

"Can I really be feeling like this already with a man I have only just met?"

Slowly the tree line started to disappear and wide open sun drenched fields opened up a vista fit for a painter, her new found feeling of content was an invigorating feeling, but she couldn't help reflecting on the excitement she felt when she had, hit the Neanderthal and Dan had beaten him to a bloody mess;

"Why did that excite her? How did it excite her? What hidden dark inner feeling of pain had awoken to allow that experience to become a pleasure?"

As the sun hung low, the warmth was fading and the breeze slowly turned cold, it was time to look for a place to stay, a place to explore what was developing, Joanne's feelings were growing stronger with every mile. A heavy mix of happiness and trepidation coupled with the feeling of excitement, what a confused polar opposite mess her head was in..... But she liked it. She thought, for the past few years, she had been 'dead' she had existed with no life, just a mundane and repetitive cycle with no joy excitement or danger, no life at all! She had lived more today than the last 10 years!

The sun was slowly dropping onto the horizon, Dan felt the grip of his new curiosity loosen as she relaxed, he is curious to where this is going?.:

"Is this fun? Is this more what I feel?"

Till he knows what it is he will feel nothing, a hardened impregnable exterior shrouding a soft delicate interior. The smell of the open countryside flooded deep into his inner core, creating a feeling of home, this is where he was happiest and on this black winding road rolling past the huge expanse of nothing, home is definitively what he felt. The mix of crops and fallow rolling past with cattle slowly munching away, horses galloping with the wild glee only an animal can have, the birds flocking in the sky, creating patterns never seen before, unique to that second, unique and of the moment. That is what he was about, that was his relaxing moment, this was his peace! With that, the desire to stop and rest came about, which was a rare feeling that did not come easy for a man who craved a three-figure heartbeat.

CHAPTER 3:

ALL ROADS LEAD TO ONE

As the day neared its end and slowly shrouded a subtle orange and red sky, the light was beautiful and yet haunting, it created a sense of hope, content and worry all rolled into one. Sat in the comfort of the big rocking chair of a motorbike, watching the world roll by as Dan did all the work, Joanne felt a flurry of warmth moving around her body, stirring her very inner life force, touching her in ways she had never been touched, stirring and bubbling inside her giving opposing feelings as pain and pleasure but those opposites seemed to complement each other. Joanne's life force was ignited with fear and excitement, she was metaphorically rebirthing from her boring life, a divergence, splitting the dull waitress with no desire or thrills to the intensity and uncertainty of her new existence.

The tranquillity was suddenly broken by the scream of high revving engines as a couple of bikes pass the comfort of the big thumping rocking chair of a bike, shocking the pair of them. The bikes pass closely, their riders baiting Dan into a 'race'. Keeping such a big bike two up on winding roads, anywhere close to two lightweight cafe racer bikes with 500 cc twin engines was not going to be easy, Dan had to be using the bike to its fullest potential, powering out of bends, flat out on the straight, at the next bend braking hard then slow in to the corner, full power out, connecting each movement with precision and experience. Each straight reigned in the little cafe racers and each bend left his monster behind. The mainly wide sweeping roads of the A6 allowed Dan to keep gaining on them as all three of them chased the sunset along an old empty road, Joanne relaxed into the flow of the 'race' feeling secure and excited in her new '*no fucks will be given*' outlook on life. Her trust was high for Dan but her lack of fear was her lack of care for herself, lack of self-regard, even self-preservation. Maybe her thought 'if we crash and burn' was actually part of the excitement, maybe feeling the danger is actually knowing you're alive? Really feeling that she was living, her heart pumping hard, flooding her body with adrenaline coupled with a chaser of fear, the concoction irresistible ravaging her body giving an extreme conflict of feelings. It was engulfing her very being and like any dominant and submissive sex relationship she was submerged in that bitter, sweet, toxic, pain and pleasure, a fear and excitement cocktail, the hedonistic mix of crazy emotions all went nicely hand in hand to heighten the experience, creating a tingling of excitement and a sickness, emotions which battled to find the most dominant.

Never had her experience felt so high! Never had she felt so alive, never had she felt so excited mentally, physically and sexually. All that was missing was a soundtrack in the back ground of an old school rock and roll band, bass, drums, rough vocals with a sweet, lead guitar. As the bike leaned from corner to corner Dan kept close enough to launch a surprise on these little pocket rockets, accelerating up behind them as the road rises, the road is about to teach, to show not everything is cut and dried, these little pocket rockets would run out of torque up the hill, Dan sunk over his fuel tank, his pillion princess pressing into his back, feeling the warmth of security from her black knight astride his black steed, transmitting a magical closeness to him. Resting herself on his strong back as the bike vibrated through both of them as one, Dan engaged full power, the huge engine blasting up the hill, tearing along the tarmac, his bike roaring and vibrating, giving so much raw torque that the rear tyre struggled for grip, trying to spin, rocketing them forward, creating a blur of scenery that dulled into just green bits and black bits.

As the huge rear wheel tamed the torque, the sides of his vision dimed the 'speed hole' in Dan's vision looking straight ahead became smaller and the two mini pocket slowed as they climbed the hill, slowing down, losing momentum despite fully open throttles, whilst the full fat terrific torque monster flew past, leaving them in a power haze as Dan crested the hill with the front wheel just lifting of the ground, a visceral display of superior torque and raw power, looking in the mirrors he viewed the two pocket rockets falling back in the distance. Dan felt Joanne gripping him as if he was a pillow on a cold lonely night, tight but soft, cuddling everything that was important to her right now.

As he shut the throttle and slowed his huge bike, the two hearts beat as one, fast, hard and happy, still completely joined in a threesome of power, danger and something Joanne could not explain. She had never felt so close to anyone, no man had ever enticed her mind so much, safe but dangerous, rough yet smooth, a mix she could not resist. Her head was a myriad of things but all the feelings were highways into happiness. She was in the moment and loving life no with plan, no cares and *'no fucks to be given'*, being on the back of a speeding bike and having full trust in her new found 'knight'. However the trust she has for Dan felt deeper than just the *'live fast die fast'* mentality, a yearning to never leave his side, a desire to be everything to him and for him, to join and be one.

As the two other bikes eventually slid past they both saluted, giving respect, never did they think the old, two up cruiser would stand a chance. As they pulled into a bike packed car park, Dan decided to turn in and follow them in to the pub a party and bonfire in full flight, more bikes doing burn outs, crotch rocket racer wannabes doing wheelies, a mix of tyre smoke and petrol. Dan was in his element, Dan followed the two little racers into the car park, they quickly park and started preening moustaches and hair, not something Dan was used to, hair products and appearance were very low on his list. He leaned back and said to his princess;

"This is as good a place any to stay I think!"

Joanne almost screamed her reply;

"Wow what a fucking rush, the best head rush ever, this is mental"

Dan smiled and gave her a small nodding motion thinking;

"That is just my norm, I bet this will be her first wild night on the road........is she feeling free? Maybe this is the start of something more for her, maybe she is truly free of her old life, if anything will set her free it will be an old school biker bash."

Walking up to the beer tent stepping over people, round people dodging beer cans and the mayhem of a wild party in full swing. Everything seemed to be happening at once, in a wild and dramatic, over the top way, people lay on the floor smoking joints, people laughing and falling over drunk, a band playing in the field, people on bikes towing drunkards on planks of wood across the grass, possessing a general freedom to do whatever they pleased. Joanne was shocked, after many years of serving coffee, paying bills and not much else she couldn't comprehend the scene;

"It's like you see in the films"

Dan winked at her with a wry smile and walked straight to the bar, saying in the manly polite way he had;

"A bottle of Whiskey, two glasses and a big fuck off cigar please!"

He was so free and she felt it, but now she was way out of her comfort zone, feeing timid and clinging close to him, needing to be protected and guided.

Sipping her whiskey back, the sharpness gave her a sensation of recoil that made her nipples hurt and her stomach tense, unsure if she liked the thought of her hard nipples or her excited feeling more, or the maybe the feeling of both! She started to drink and the mind-numbing sharpness, filled her with confidence again, her heart racing as she wandered over to two guys drinking shots out of a woman's belly, the woman enjoying the attention as much as the men enjoying licking a liquor covered woman's body.

The drunken, bearded, topless men high on lust, shots and whatever else they could get their hands on taking it in turns to drink from the woman's semi-naked body, lying in just a bra and denim cut-off shorts, the cut so high they were barely covering anything. Nobody had any inhibitions, nobody wanted anyone else's approval and nobody cared if you didn't like what they did or how they looked. The old school bikers made the two pansy hair product guys on the café racers look out of place. The air was filled with lust, laughter and freedom to do whatever they wanted.

Joanne actually had no idea what she was going to do as she slowly walked up to them, nobody had even noticed this

English rose almost floating into the mix and with that, she pulled open her press stud uniform pushed her shot glass in between her breasts and let the two bikers wrestle and push each other to one side to get to it. The two were one step away from a full on battle, feet slipping on the grass and dragging each other back, determined to get to her and drink from her pushed up breasts.

She loved the feeling of having her semi-dressed body ogled by many, she looked over at Dan who raised his glass, took a large puff of his cigar and winked at her. It drove her wild. Making her more daring and freeing her of social constraint!

As she hopped on to the table and lay back the nerves bubbled slightly as she looked around, everyone cheering and shouting with big drunken smiles, they lined up the shots on her belly, then tipping them over, the coldness making her jump, which wobbled her breasts as if trying to tease the baying revellers. The two guys started sucking and licking the drinks from her body, more and more people men and women joining in, taking their turn on the new English rose that had blossomed in front of them, it was driving her crazy making her wet in so many ways.

Sipping the whiskey and puffing his cigar Dan stands hard and erect mentally physically and sexually, stood with the pride and command of a lion looking over his playful pride of lions. Looking like a man who could burst into action at any time, ready for love or war. His desires ravishing the fabric of his being, creating a den of iniquity in his head and a powerful desire to get fucked blued and tattooed, the joining of them both was stretching and pushing each other, completing each other's needs and taking them to places unknown.

Dan casually walked over, placing his over-full glass on her chest, he poured the whiskey between her breasts, the cold trickle sending goose bumps over her flesh as he chased the whiskey down between her breasts with his tongue, tracing across her ribs down her soft and cute stomach, flicking his tongue in her belly button, her body shook and her breasts wobbled inside that black and white bra for all to see and with one last crescendo, Dan flicked his tongue over her pants, burying his head between her legs sucking her whiskey soaked pants, sucking so hard on her clitoris through her silky black and white ribbon pants, she was close to a very fast orgasm. The crowd watching and cheering has actually turned her on more than Dan; he shook his head side to side rubbing his face against her pussy till, she screamed. No one even hears her as the onlookers cheer louder than the band are playing, drowning out her wild bucking and quivering orgasmic screams, watching her writhing on the table, completely in a world of her own, a world with Dan's face buried between her legs.

With a look of pride he smiled at the pack of drunken voyeurs, scooped her up and gave her a drink, he walked with her back to the bar, her head feeling like it was bouncing and her body still shaking, as if she was 10 feet tall. People were slapping them on the back and clapping, heightening the feeling, fulfilled by the voyeuristic accolade of an orgasm in full view of a group.

A 20's something girl with a flower behind her ear and a look of the 60's rushed up grabbing them both by the arm with a drunken chaotic look in her face;

"Wow just wow you two are amazzzzzzing"

Her long blonde natural hair tamed by a retro bandana, her clothes all flowing and bright;

"You two are the hottest thing I have ever seen. You're old, yet free spirited, I want to be you guys, I want to be you and be part of you. Are you camping here?"

"Kinda!"

Dan exclaimed with the cigar between his teeth;

"I have no tent but will sleep under the stars!"

"No way you're staying with me tonight, my tents more like a tepee, you have to meet everyone! They will love you!"

As she flowed, skipped and twirled,

"My name is Indy"

The 20 something hippy styled girl stated, almost singing the words as she smiled and floated around them.

"Follow me. Come, come"

The words are melodic and dancing around their ears luring them into her merriment, she grabbed Dan and Joanne and led them through the crowds, dodging the revellers and performers, skilfully ducking and weaving around trumpets and banners.

The truth was both Dan and Joanne struggled to keep up, her delicate but vice like grip kept them tracking behind her, intoxicated by the smells of hog roast, beer, skunk and poppers. Joanne was lost in a mix of post orgasmic voyeurism and the confusion from a variety of smells and noise, the heady mix from the crowds and the music from the marching bands all dressed up in in red jackets and white trousers. Joanne was stunned, never had she seen such opposites, clean cut marching bands and heavy metal bands setting up on stage, people who look like they would melt if it rained and people who looked like they would scare Satan himself, all roaming in the same space sharing the same enjoyment.

Suddenly they appeared out of the crowd to a group of tents of all sizes, yet one large colourful tent with smoke spiralling from the hole in the top, this had to be the one Indy was in! She rushed in interrupting all the drunken meandering conversation;

"You have to meet these two. They are sooooooooo offfff the chain they are yanking it themselves!"

With a few murmurs and awkward hellos from everyone, Indy bursts into a story of two old lovers who have been together for decades embracing their sexuality in front of everyone drinking shots of her body and teasing each other;

"It was so beautttttttiiiiiiiffffffuuuuullll"

Dan boldly interrupted;

"We have only known each other a few hours"

"No way!!!"

She cried, flicking her long blond hair out of her face;

"You guys are totally connected like before you even met, you're like past life lovers or something".

A clean cut 60 something thin guy stood up, wearing turned up drain pipe jeans and a tight white top with his hair greased but slowing falling from its set place to one side, he ran his fingers through it and took a draw from a small joint;

"Indy get these two a drink and I think another for yourself!"

He laughed;

"I am Benjie, this is Emily my wife"

He pointed to a slim woman lay on some large bean bags, wearing very tight leather jeans and a low cut (literally cut from the neck with a pair of scissors) top exposing her large breasts, contained by some tour tee shirt band from a generation long forgotten;

"This is Jack"

Benjie pointed to the man leaning against the centre pole, with a short beard, a bit of a belly and a look of a man who might hug you or kill you, with no in-between;

"The flashy guy on the chair is Bradley"

Benjie waved his hand towards the man, dressed in all new gear branded and all matching (a bit of a dealership queen with lots of cash and an equally huge watch)

"And last but not least little Ritchie..........he is the rally virgin feel free to abuse him as much as you like!"

Ritchie not even fazed by what was said lifted up his hand, pretending to tip his forelock at the two; Dan was ultimately impressed by a young man with respect and old school manners.

Indy floated back in between them, handing them a couple of cans of beer, pulled them over to a large pile of cushion, she started talking even before they were sat;

"We are heading up to a rally in some little place called Helmand but we can't find it on the map!"

Dan smiled and pulled a cigarette from his pocket, lit up it and after a large cloud of smoke chased its way above his head and out to the top of the tepee he said;

"Do you mean Helmsley? That's a rally I have been to many times.......I think Helmand is in Afghanistan, I was there a few years ago"

Dealership queen spat his fine Belgian ale all over himself as he muttered;

"What the actual fuck? We have been looking for a war zone! That's what you get when you let a flower girl do the planning. For fucks sake give me that map!"

Joanne could see Dan on the verge of boiling as he stared at this pansy biker with pitch perfect everything; she pulled his hand close to her and kept it taut, before Dan could do anything. A growled voice, so low it reverberated and scraped down your back, came from the other side of the tent;

"Watch your fucking mouth rich boy, she is not one of your cling-on trophy girls. You treat her with respect or I will fucking rip that smarmy look from your face!"

Now there was a man Dan could associate with, Jack was about 50, *'mean as fuck'*, but in possession of more respect and morals than most, the thought that this was the type of person Dan should actually be around gently flourished through his mind, the tension in his body melted and he leaned back smoking his cigarette. He said calmly in a deep voice;

"Helmsley is about 10 miles-ish from where I grew up."

Indy jumped to her feet;

"Well that's it you must come with us and we can follow you"

As Dan lay in his own smoke, sipping his beer with nothing but a bunch of strangers, he felt a belonging, a sense of completion, something that he had been missing for many years, the feeling was slowly filling a void in his cold dark existence, the figures and faces around him drifted away with the smoke becoming clouds. This was reality, this was life, this was success! When all felt black he had found a ray of sunshine, a purpose and a belonging.

"Where next mister Lone Wolf? Is this your pack? Is this your herd? Or are we all actually loners just finding solitude in others when we need it?"

His inner voice knew exactly how to tear through Dan, striking the calmness from his demeanour, rushing him to control his fits of rage and more often than not his self-loathing.

Dan's feeling of content was very short lived and the darkness of his mind evolved and encapsulated his thoughts;

"Are we pack animals or are we all meant to be loaners? Why do some crave more attention than others? Are we actually "lone packers", a species that needs both a pack and solitude? Are we actually trying too hard to stay in the pack when we may need some lone wolf time, to get our mind together and find our true guiding spirt that is so downtrodden by the noise of the herds?"

Dan's constant revelations of himself and life, continued to shape him, kept him positive, temporarily lifting the dark mental shroud that often cloaked his questioning mind, keeping him in check and constantly trying to better himself, tortured by the things he saw wrong with himself, but equally enlightened by the things he improved about himself. The desire for betterment would never end for Dan as more revelations brought more questions and improvement.

Floating over with her flowery gown and blonde hair Indy slipped in between Dan and Joanne, her presence pushing away any negativity floating around Dan;

"I meant what I said you two should come with us, I so much want what you have"

She put her hands on both of their thighs;

"I want to be you and I want you!"

Joanne looks over and winked;

"I like her, she will be fun!"

Dan's three figure heart beat returned pulsing blood round his body, raising his temperature and turning his cerebral mind into a frenzy engulfing his body with more endorphins than he could handle.

Trying to control the frenzy his thoughts turned to;

"How can an old guy like me, washed up, skint and worthless actually end up with such a leading light to my life? Direction from nothing, light from darkness, happiness and excitement from despair, how did this even happen? Keeping momentum and moving forward, never giving up that's how!"

This felt to Dan like some kind of utopian religious order, but a religious man he was not, what was this? What had caused me to keep moving forward, ending up with a group of like mind people and a curvy sexy woman and a young slim hippy wanting a threesome, could his life get any better?

Indy flowing and dancing led them off to another tent, with many blankets cushions, flowers and red velvet interior, a dim light hanging from the top and a sweet smell of burnt sage.

"This is my tent, I hired it for me, I sometimes need to recharge and not be with the rest of the group, often I need some solitude and space. Sometimes I need a select couple to enjoy too"

She giggled, the wayward happy nature of Indy was so intoxicating to Dan who casually threw his leather jacket in the corner. Wearing his trademark white tight vest top and black jeans, he stands surveying the moment as if a lion with his lionesses, his muscular shoulders, back and strong chest protruding, tapering in a 'V' to his waist. Indy flowed across the tent, her hippy clothes trailing behind her, revealing a slender thigh as she moved like a ballet dancer to a large pile of oversize cushions and fur throws, Joanne slightly more tense and still in her uniform with a need for some clothes that are more appropriate for the bike. With her new-found lust and care free life, she slowly moved across to the furs and looked over at Dan and with a wink she knelt down to Indy and kissed her on the lips then ran her fingers through Indy's curly blonde hair.

Dan's heart is three figures multiple times over, once again, adrenaline rampaging through his body, the excitement of an old man getting exactly what he wanted!

Indy and Joanne rolled around passionately and playfully kissed, running fingers through each other's hair, biting licking and dragging nails down each other's backs, Indy dropped her bright flowing clothes off her shoulder, revealing a slim tanned body with small pert breasts, her lack of any underwear momentarily shocked Joanne, Indy leaned forward and started to kiss down Joanne's body, stripping her of her uniform and revealing her curvy, well-used bod, Indy exclaimed;

"I wish I had your body."

Dan moved forward, wide eyed and gleefully looking at the two opposites that are Indy and Joanne;

"I wish I had both your bodies"

With a giggle, Dan is pulled in by the waistband of his jeans, dropping to his knees in front of the two women who he already adores, this momentary feeling more perfect than any other he had been in before, his steady smooth way not failing him, confidence carrying him through the moment, he kissed Joanne with a prowess, a confidence, a love maybe? He turned to Indy who practically eats him alive, her legs and arms wrapped around him her breasts trapped against his strong chest, she pulled Joanne in and whispered;

"Who should go first?"

Joanne wasted no time pulling out his cock and before Indy can react she devoured it, using her hand to extenuate her motions, proving her experience and demonstrating that age has a huge advantage over youth, she turned to Indy and with a wry smile they both descend on Dan toying with him kissing each other playing with him and playing with each other, clearly this was not Indy's first threesome.

Dan fell on his back with his jeans just low enough for his huge throbbing erection to be fully out, Joanne moves over and lowered her curvy bum onto his bearded face making his beard wet, showing how turned on she is, he grabbed her bum and pulled her tighter onto his face, licking, sucking and fingering her, Indy moved over and slowly lowers herself on to him, allowing the tip of his cock to rub against her till she slides down taking him fully inside her, controlling his manhood using him as she needs taking what she wants and how she wants it, feeling empowered and lighter than air. Dan shook and moaned, the vibrations from his mouth exciting Joanne more.

The two women were now fully in control of Dan, they moved on to each other whilst still astride him, skilfully writhing on top of Dan, having their fun from Dan whilst taking more from each other, teasing each other, hands everywhere, taking their multiple orgasms to a place only possible in a threesome and by the skilful encounter of woman on woman, riding a man till he could take no more. The three of them collapsed into an erotic orgasmic pile, with the wonderful post sex feeling, they all lay there breathing heavy and feeling light headed with the typical musky smell ravishing them.

It felt like hours that they had all lay there, just running their fingers over every inch of each other's bodies while their minds slowly returned, kissing licking and stroking from head to toe, whilst their bodies tingled with delight. None of them were aware of anything other than the moment they were in, the perfect state of an idealistic moment, no past no future just the present, totally relaxed and quiet minds, no searching, no moving forward just peace.

CHAPTER 4:

DANGEROUS LIAISONS

Dan awoke with a smile, content and calmness filling his mind. The velvet interior of the tent keeping it dark and safe, wrapping him safely from the world in his den of iniquity, the sweetness of the sage and smell of happiness evoked a calming sensation, one Dan recognised but was not overly familiar with.

Dan still felt the burning need to roam, he got up and headed out with vest and jeans on, carrying his black and heavily aged leather jacket under his arm, walking through the array of tents, not actually going anywhere, just roaming and sensing the calm and happiness, comforting but odd, these feelings that did not feel natural to a man who lived in search of excitement. The tents were surrounded by the aftermath of a party; one Dan was at but actually not, as he'd spent most of the night covered in two women. The thought brought a small, slow smile crept across his face; the sun starting to sneak through the clouds warmed his very soul. Nobody was out of a tent anywhere, just Dan, as he wandered through the mixture of bottles, cans and smouldering barbecues.

Nothing intrigued him enough to hold his interest or desire, nothing could hold his mind, he hoped this rally was as good as it used to be. It was time to get the others Dan needed to ride!

Walking into the tent Indy and Joanne were sprawled on the bed of cushions and coloured voiles, Indy with one leg exposed from a blanket and a single breast belonging to Joanne just starting to peek out, the memories of last night and the smell of women on his beard teased his nostrils as he moved, he casually knocked over a bottle with just enough noise to wake them up. Seeing them smile in the morning light that was protruding through the doorway, illuminating them like angels, Joanne spoke;

"Well you're up and about early, Mr 'Whatever else you can give me'!"

Dan didn't even look up at her, just a gruff voice and a half smile;

"Yep, time to pack up"

"But I only have my uniform I think I need some proper gear"

Indy stretched, revealing more of her long, slender legs, tantalising long and inviting;

"We can fix that, I know a guy with too much kit. Let's get you sorted! Bradley has way too much stuff, he will have multiple jackets and gear. Let's go and raid those huge panniers he brings just so he can change jackets and boots throughout the weekend like some kind of fashion parade."

Dan felt the bite of rage, enjoying anything to wipe his smarmy smile off Bradley's face, maybe even burn all his gear, the thought trampled through his brain, stamping on rational thoughts crushing them and taking over, the older Dan got, the harder he was finding it to keep his calm and his fists in check. Or perhaps he just no longer cared.

The three of them ran over to Bradley's bike, Indy straight away started pulling out multiple garments and a sweet, open face helmet, painted in black and red glitter flake;

"Here try this and this, they will all work nice."

Joanne pulled on the padded jeans, they were a bit tight as she stretched them around her pear shaped figure, she caught both Dan and Indy looking at her bum and with a smile the memories of last night all came flooding back, second hand waves of ecstasy drowning her insecurities and making her feel sexy, Indy threw her a top with a skull and a crystal ball and finally a leather jacket, trying it on she struggled to get her zip up over her chest but the two smiles watching her, made her not care. She felt desired and sexy, rocking the tight, biker gear look, hugging every curve;

"How do I look?"

Indy giggled.

"Like we she should take you back to bed"

As they walked into the tepee the others were just packing up, Emily looked them up and down with a gentle knowing and said to Benjie;

"Just like the good old days of our youth. I miss the 60's, we ruled the waves and spent many nights on the beaches."

She winked at him and carried on packing her bag. Dealer boy Bradley started immediately;

"Hey nice jacket. I have one just like it."

Indy hid her snigger as she skipped around, floating from person to person giving snippets of last night's little ménage a trois. Dan was feeling uncomfortable now, itchy feet, time to move, packed with only the clothes on his back and his duffel bag he had not even opened;

"I will wait for you out front"

Dan strode off alone, strong, independent, untouchable and unavailable, needing solitude and a place to be, leaving on his black mistress with a cigarette between his teeth he felt safe, the urge to leave alone strong but under control. Held by something, or someone, something was happening, he actually cared, he felt attached and weighted to something he could not fight. His itchy feet were driving him crazy, why were they taking so long?

Ritchie the rally virgin arrived first strapping his stuff to a super moto, predictably, Dan mused. Jack the bad ass biker in old boots, heavily worn jeans a black tee and a Nomad rocker patch on his cut, surely that old 'Shovel Head' next to Richie's was 'Mr Bad Ass Biker's?' Sure enough, he straddled across the old custom chopper, put his feet on his girder forks and lit a smoke. Never has someone looked so content with his life. Dan's inner questions now strangely playful;

"Could I actually guess all of their bikes? Would they have guessed my black mistress was mine?"

The old rocker couple Benji and Emily walked over, sharing the weight of the bags. Clearly that genuine old café racer had to be theirs. Sure enough, they strapped their well-packed luggage to a pristine, black and chrome 60's beauty. Bradley the dealership bro was already known, that just left Indy, which bike would be hers? Scouring the array of bikes, he spotted a traditional white and purple chopper with skinny seat and tall sissy bar, straight out of *'Easy Rider'*. That had to be it, as she danced and pranced her away across to the bikes, the weird excitement of guessing the bikes had captivated Dan, sure enough she strapped her stuff on the seat of the 70's chopper, without a care in the world, a mix of bikers from different worlds all coming together as one. For Dan this is what bikes were about; individuals, personalities, all able to express themselves without the fear of criticism, apart from the dealer prick that deserved it, not a real bike man just a guy with a wallet who thinks he is cool with high end fashion clothes. Anywhay where was he and what was taking him so long?

"Dealer bro" walks over to his bike and started to put a bag in one of his panniers. Before he even got his bag near to the bike, Dan's bike roared into life, shaking and burbling through a short straight piped exhaust. Blipping the throttle and scanning for his curvy intrigue, he watched her stride over like a modern day Olivia Newton John, just missing the phrase; *'Tell me about it stud!'* Dan's ego roared louder than his bike, his heart smashing against his rib cage aching with desire and a hard on that drove him insane.

Joanne hopped on the back of the engine with a seat and bars (it was more engine than it was bike). Ripping the throttle back, spinning the rear wheel in the dirt he launched the bike forward. Thoughts raged through Dan's cerebral cortex, all coming together in an egotistical explosion of emotions, the only words that rampaged into his mind were;

"MOTHERFUCKER! FUCKING FUCK YEAH!"

Dan's mind was akin to a man jumping out of a helicopter with a cigar in his mouth, a machine gun in hand and dropping behind enemy lines. The others tore after him, their wheels stirring up a dust cloud so thick dealership bro would need a week of cleaning on his immaculate chromed bike.

Dan was a mental mess, confused, stressed, anxious, excited, happy and sad all at once. Happiness and content did this to him, never knowing if he was coming or going. So going it was, the only way he knew how to, exercising his demons with his fist tightly wrapped around his throttle and his well-worn boot clicking through the gears.

Winding himself into the road, listing to the Almighty, his Master, his Maker, his deity, his saviour, his mixed up well of emotions still tormented him, hurting his head and tearing a strip from his mortal soul as he battled with his life of pain, that he would rather keep buried than allow back to the surface.

Skimming the road on his beautiful black beauty, with a beautiful woman at his back, a row of bikes following in his wake, raging or not, he felt on top of the world, the cars on the road, the herds of 'norms' going about their normal day, drifted into an insignificant place in Dan's head.

Checking his mirror to look for his little pack he saw a flash of red. Dan looked up and viewed the car heading for impact with them, the car was swerving towards them. As the young lad drove, the little red car crossed the white line into Dan's lane. With his phone in one hand and the other on the steering wheel, the driver was looking down at his phone unaware he was about to kill someone with his clapped-out banger of a car! Dan swerved away, narrowly missing the car, coming close to colliding with the front of the car, tucking his leg in and hoping to avoid the devastating impact. Manhandling his huge behemoth trying to avoid losing control, swerving away from the kerb and getting it straight, he looked in his mirror to see the car mount the kerb as the café racer with Benjie and Emily on swerved onto the wrong side of the road narrowly missing multiple cars. Benjie, lost control of the bike, shiny black and chrome down on the ground, sliding with the bike resting on him, and Emily rolled down the road like a rag doll, arms and legs flailing in the air in a super 'slow motion' roll.

"FOR FUCKS SAKE! LITTLE ARROGANT PRICK!"

Dan locked his rear wheel, screeching to a stop, spun his bike round and roared back towards the scene, his tyre ripping up stones from the hot tarmac, flinging them backwards in a battle between, smoke, rubber and tarmac. He slammed on the brakes and ordered Joanne;

"Check they are okay!"

She jumped off the bike, shaken and nearly in tears, with a feeling of sickness and horror ravaging her. Dan spun the rear wheel, leaving a black line on the road fishtailing left and right, filling the air with smoke heavier than his mood, he screamed at the driver as he dragged his bars down the side of the car, now two wheels on the kerb. Dropping the stand and cutting the engine off, Dan banged his fists on the car as he ran round to the driver's side like a silverback gorilla, circling the car, pounding it as he ran around to the driver's side of the car, he threw an almighty punch through the open driver's window, glancing the guy's cheek, not fully connecting.

Dan snatched the phone from his hand as he leaned into the car; he smelled the alcohol and saw the half-drunk vodka bottle, resting in the lap of the driver.

A three figure heartbeat, mixing with three figure rage, coupled with his confused state of emotions he had tried to lock up in his mind, he burst with anger, trying to drag the driver through the open window, but he still had his seat belt on. Dan yanked him by his clothes half out of his seat banging his head against the side of the car. The driver's torso was only partially out of the window when Dan leapt up in the air and brought both fists down on to the side of the driver's head, bending his neck more than 90 degrees against the car door, the cracking noise reverberated from the car metal work, the noise lingered in the air, slicing through the onlookers with a medieval style horror, the noise made everyone wince, as the noise trickled past everyone's ears, touching them in a way that caused a cold sensation to run down their spines.

The pack were no longer merry. Instead, very sombre, all crowded around Benji and Emily who were now lifting the bike up and checking it over. Dan continued to beat the lifeless body still hanging half out the car, each blow splashing more crimson revenge over his face.

As the driver's torso hung from the car window Dan slowly lifted his head and looked towards the group, who all just stared at him in shock, mouths open in horror as Dan's blood-splattered face emerged into view above the car. He was holding the driver's phone in one hand and the half empty vodka bottle in the other. A sickening feeling crept into the whirling mess of his stomach, sorrow, fear, anger all swishing around him, crushed and broken with repentance, a lump harder than a golf ball in his throat slowly choking him for the murderous act of revenge.

Benji stared into the eyes of a man whose face is splattered with blood, he looked tortured, sorry and fearful and he took the bottle and phone from Dan;

"You're a noble man, you're a protector, a born leader and I thank you for your solidarity for my wife and I, but you cannot wait around you need to disappear, we will stand by you, you are our brother! A Viking of a man......but for now though you are, for whom the bell tolls"

Benjie turned to the group still holding the bottle of vodka and phone, lifting them high for everyone to see as if an offer to a God;

"We ride with our brother equal in all measures, we protect him with the same severity that he has used to avenge the wrong done against us, we ride as one a solid pack......so start your engines and let's get to safety this could be a messy few days!"

The mood was different now, no smiles, no playful riding, no high revs or burnouts, no waves, salutes or horn beeping, just a slow departure slipping away in to the road. As they all rode away from the execution of a young man who died for his stupidity, just a group surrounding a blood-stained Neanderthal's honour, a man struggling to keep his mind together, as he battled with the harsh truth of what he had done.

"Why do I go so far? Why do I feel so much anger? Why can't I stop this cyclical return to the dark side?

The miles clicked by as they left the main roads, Indy riding with horror in her heart, a feeling changed from seeing Dan as the almighty protector to the brutal and nasty thug. Feelings she may never be able to live with, the brutality she has witnessed, the vision of an execution that may never leave her, stained into her mind. The whole group is traumatised by the experience, not knowing what to do, they were witnesses and would they be seen as accomplices? Dan edged his bike in front leading them through this ribbon of hope, looking for the light and looking for the direction of his life. Weaving from small country road to small country road, Dan felt like he was being watched, even the trees seemed to glare at him with disgust for the grotesque violence of his reaction, Dan's deep thoughts toyed with him;

"Are you as wrong as the driver was? Who are you? A murderer? A thug? Avenging angel? Or Lucifer himself?"

Dan can barely concentrate when a sign leading to the rally loomed into view, the pack surrounding him, showing their strength. Jack worked his old school 'Shovel Head' through the pack, drawing alongside Dan he pointed to himself and waves to the group in a *'no worries'* motion, taking control and illustrating the need to trust him. Jack pulled out in front of the pack, the rough noise of his old V twin clattering away and the now painfully obvious leather cut and nomad rocker on his back; he passed the entrance to the rally, the sun dropping below the tree line and a steady flow of bikes entering the site.

As Jack pulled up in a gateway full of security, the largest of the security group shouted;

"The entrance is back there! You can't get in here!"

Jack slowly rode up to the man who started to recognise his old mate. After some back-slapping hugs and laughter, there were some two-way radio conversations and some awkward looks, the group were all feeling very odd. Dan started to protect himself and turn his emotions stone like, he tried to forget as much detail as possible and stook his chin out like a proud man, whilst his relentless mind fought with him;

"Who actually am I? A thug or a hero? A criminal or a judge? Who actually am I to judge anyone?"

Jack waved them all down to the side gate which is now opened just for them;

"He owes me some favours and we have a no questions asked window to merge and disappear into the crowds, Dan you need to get cleaned up you look like you're on way to a Halloween party."

Jack was often a man of few words but every word counted!

They all slowly rode in, joining the trail of bikes entering the site. The rally was a wonderful debauchery of decadence and shameless behaviour. It felt like home to all of them, a freedom of the road and likeminded people, living a *'no fucks given'* kind of life. Being here with all these folk, was for them, like taking medicine, recharging their darkened souls, like healing had begun.

The group descended onto a patch of grass near a tap with a very downbeat mood, all parked and quiet, amongst the pandemonium of people who were arriving and starting to party, opening cans of beer even before they put the tent up. One guy, on a huge cruiser with a bat wing faring had a bottle of beer in a holder on his bars, he rumbled past, laughing and cheering to everyone as he passed through, looking for a place to camp. However, the group stared, unsure how to start after the mess left behind on the road. Ritchie got off his super moto and sat on the grass, cracking a beer open out of his rucksack and steadily he started to drink, raising his can, but no words come out of his open mouth, his youth and inexperience shinning brighter than ever. Bradley climbed off his bling, custom painted metal flake dealership queen bike, unusually lost for words, looking around, searching for a word, any word. Jack lit up a cigarette, he leaned against his old school 'Shovel Head'. As he looked around the group he started a speech with a deep, quiet, precise and clear voice;

"This man comes into our lives with high morals and even higher disgust for the entitled generation.....we the forgotten generation should stand by him, he is a warrior and a loyal man who has protected, guided and feels love for us like a family, his first thought was to stop by you two on the road, leaving Joanne to tend to you, while he took care of business, he is an old school biker with respect, loyalty and values, a true friend who will stand and fight for you when you can no longer fight, a man who in my book has done nothing wrong, that little shit deserved it and had I have been

closer to the car I would have done the same! I stand by you my brother and so should all of you! If any of you disagree, fuck you and fuck the entitled generation, pack up your bike and leave. However remember; you breathe a word to anyone and we all owe Dan now, especially you two old rockers, when you lay on the floor he came back for you! I will bury anyone who talks about this to the law or media!"

For a man of normally so few words, his clear and lengthy speech had a mixed effect, most were starting to smile and nod, Bradley who was sitting on his bike felt sick, reliving the horrific moment when a man was executed for his stupidity, without judge or jury, the hairs on his neck still raised his heart racing as his hands still shaking, Jack slowly sauntered over to him, with a walk that belonged in a John Wayne western;

"What's it gonna be posh boy? Are you with us or without us? Time to be a real biker and support your new brother, or pack up that huge dealer queen of yours and ride till you forget our names!"

Bradley raised his head and looked Jack square in the eye with all the promise of a man but not feeling anything like a man, his stomach turning knots, trying to hold back the vomit in his throat that burned his throat as it climbed into his mouth. He swallowed hard and said;

"I stand with you, but I will be honest, I thought I would kick ass if something like this happened but I froze and I am sorry"

The cocky nature of Bradley was gone his voice humble and head hung low with the realisation he is no better than anyone else. He was a judgemental guy and now was judging himself for not stepping up, for not being the big man he thought he was, the pain in his own head was excruciating, a mix of self-loathing and sorrow dragged him down.

Jack opened his bottle of whiskey and took a large slug of it, passing it to Bradley;

"Here, this will straighten you out."

Offering the bottle at Bradley's face, without even looking at him, he took it and gulped a large mouthful, gasping and almost choking, Jack smiled;

"Everyone is on a journey, this is yours and your posh boy name no longer suits you, for this journey your name is Blockhead like that engine of yours, you are one of us now, that means equal not above or below, equal!"

"Blockhead I quite like that"

With that he started unpacking his stuff from his large panniers, for a moment there is a double take when he searched for stuff that was missing, he looked up at Joanne, smiles and said;

"It looks better on you anyway."

Blockhead was different, no longer acting like he owned the world and everything in it. But so was everyone, even Jack who had leapt into action just when he was needed, to sort everyone out. The tents were all pitched close together, as if trying to shield themselves, from anyone and everyone, looking like a group of Indians protecting against the cowboys, Joanne was not excited like the last time she witnessed Dan's rage and power, this time it has been different, there was no real threat to anyone just a young stupid boy who made a big mistake and now lay on a mortuary slab.

With all the tents up and offers from everyone for Dan and Joanne to sleep in their tent, Dan was humbled by the reaction of his new family, he had shown a dangerous volatile reaction, one he had to control far too frequently and this time it had escaped, uncontrolled and set free on the world. He was distant again, a thousand- yard stare with an unfocused mind. What had he done? What had he started? What would happen next?

"What the actual fuck have I done? Once again everyone will hate me for what I have done, letting the monster out from the darkest part of my soul that hates the world and everyone in it, the part just looking for a reason to escape and wreak havoc on all that have crossed me. The devil who sits inside me deserves no sympathy, no forgiveness, no second chance, a vile creature who needs to be controlled, only allowing him to inspire me in times of threat, not for some fool who nearly caused an issue, for me or people I respect!"

Benjie and Emily slowly walked over to Dan, they both put a hand on his shoulder and in unison said;

"Thank you, thanks for caring enough to stop and make sure we were okay, family is not about blood, it's about who is there to hold your hand when you need it the most, you held our hand today, thank you for doing what I wanted to do but am 20 years too old to do it. You are a bit of a bad ass, I can see though you are broken, this is not joy you have; although you do have the heart of an angel, coupled to the rage of a bear. You may have done wrong in some people's eyes, but in my day if someone did you a wrong they got a kicking, he could have killed us and you did what needed doing. We owe you anything you ask for, apart from my sweetheart she is mine and for her I will never be too old to fight"

Dan can't help a little smile creeping across his face, he nodded, and with that simply said;

"You're all good people but I need to wander. I need to collect my thoughts."

Dan bowed his head as he walked into the crowds, walking a well-trodden path in his mind, a mind as worn out as the boots he was treading across the field in, his mind worn old, scuffed but comfortable and easy to walk in, this feeling was common to him, almost comforting, as the mardi-gras of people around him moved both fast and loudly, Dan barely noticed them, they are silent to him, as if he is watching a video clip on mute, the hazy rush of people doing their thing surrounding him but not even on the same planet. Separate, just sharing the same space. As Dan trod that path well walked, he questioned;

"Why? What next? Who does this make me? Do I hate myself or love who I am? Why can't I just be normal?

As he questioned, his lips pursed, he tilted his head upwards, and a cynical smile lit up his tired old face. One question was answered, because he would be bored with normality, he would despise any repetitive life, following the rules! He needed more, he needed too feel too really feel life, not just a little bit but full fat, full caffeine full 100% feel it, like a 100 mile an hour icy wind he needed to FEEL it. That little prick had it coming, he would have killed somebody the way he was, ignorant little shit, the feeling of a raucous life bubbled up inside him from the pit of his stomach, flooding his body like a special power, and this was his special power. A vibrant energy floods through his body as his stride became more purposeful, the surroundings were turned back up unmuted and he was back in his world.

As he strode with more and more purpose he noticed his thirst, a thirst that could drink a pub bone dry, stopping at a partially set up stall he grabbed a bottle of whiskey and asked how much, the guy replied;

"£30 and coke is extra."

"Coke? No chance mate. Full flavour, no extras to water it down!"

As he paid, he chuckled to himself, full power, full on that's the only way, dark and moody with everything a different shade of black. Lots of black is like that shades of grey book only darker he laughed to him self.

Swigging from the bottle as he walked, his need to live and feel crawled up his spine reaching deep into his very core. Dan was reborn but with more, far more than before!

Joanne ran over to him;

"I was so worried about you are you okay?"

Dan noticed the sky was a deep red and yellow as the sun had dropped behind the tree line;

"You have been gone hours"

"I am fine I am always fine. In fact I am back literally and figuratively. I am back!"

The odd look in his eyes, made her unsure of whether she should actually believe him or not;

"Let's party let's get fucked blued and tattooed!"

Emily chuckled;

"Well let's get something at least".

The rally was starting to wake up, the more the sun dropped the more the noise increased, fireworks, BBQ's drag racing and more individual styled people than Joanne had ever seen, some dressed in cave man outfits some in steampunk some in wild indescribable outfits, some just naked, care free do as you want non-judgemental and free!

As the bikes raced up and down a semi hidden makeshift drag strip on a little side road of the campsite (not strictly legit at this rally) they filled the air with the perfect biker mix of petrol and burning rubber, with bikes revving off the rev limiter and popping back in the exhaust adding to the general petrol parting pandemonium, everything from single cylinder thumpers to V twin's, triples and full on race reps, with even some weird homemade crazy bikes joining the general lunacy. It was like thousands of friends all wanting the same thing had come together and with that an almighty bang, as a supercharged shed built bike, blew its engine and bucked its rider off on to the makeshift dirt runway, cheers and whoops from the crowd as he got up and the bike lay there bleeding its black and green life all over the floor, coolant and oil everywhere. No drama, no issues, no rules, just people helping him clear it to the side, as another rolled up and performed a burn out, smoke filled the air, the lights of the bikes flickering through the drifting smoke making it look even more magical. Joanne cuddled into Dan, she had never felt this kind of closeness or freedom, never had she felt life was so perfect;

"Well I was serious about fucked blued and tattooed, I am none of the above yet tonight, so what's first?"

As he swigged from the whiskey bottle she replied;

"Dan, let's do them all"

She grabbed the bottle from him and drunk the whiskey like a man, straight from the bottle, neat, just as it should be.

As they wandered from stall to stall it was clear this was a no holds barred place, a myriad of eclectic stalls as usual, with clothes, poppers, harder stuff under the counter not hidden just slightly less on view. Then she saw it;

"Look, piercing and tattoos"

Looking at all the designs to many to choose, Dan spoke;

"Can you do me a Viking helmet around my nipple?"

"Yep, grab a chair"

The tattooist, covered in piercings and 'tatts' from head to toe, wearing a kilt.

"Can't tattoo you if you have been drinking."

"No worries pal."

Dan swigged from his bottle again, the guy laughing as he started to buzz the ink around his nipple;

"Fleshy this bit, not really painful",

Joanne, curious of her new-found world asked;

"What is the most painful thing you have had done?"

The kilted man stood up, lifted up his kilt and revealed a monstrous cock with an even bigger Prince Albert;

"Well you did ask!"

Stunned with her mouth wide open, she thought of how this was so much better than her previous hum-drum life serving truckers greasy breakfasts. With the helmet tattoo finished Joanne sat and quietly said;

"It's my first one, can I just have a small moon crescent and some stars on my leg? It's my first time."

He smiled, lifting her leg the tattooist winked and said;

"It's been a long time since someone said that to me when I am between their legs"

Her giggle made he sound like a virginal 16 year old, but the memories of their escapade in Dan's mind came raging to the forefront reminding him how far removed from virginal she actually was.

The bitter sweet pain of the tattoo taking place was hard for her to explain, she wanted to have the tattoo so much yet the pain as the needle dragged across her skin, literally scarring her for life, making her unsure, was she doing the right thing? As she looked at Dan so bold and strong, so confident and at ease, not needing any approval from anyone, her desire to be tattooed pushed her through the pain, slightly sweaty and feeling a sickness that was making her wish it to be over.

As the tattooist lifted his head with a look of pride and a slight head tilt, she looked down at her new ink and instantly loved it. Knowing that all of the time before Dan, had just been waiting for him to arrive and show her a new life. A life of excitement and thrills, with no holds barred, full fat and full pace. Dan was visibly in an odd mood, a man seemingly with everything yet teetering on the edge of losing everything, how can life be so perfect yet so wrong? Wrestling with the 'Pandora's box' that is what his rage has done and what it may have caused, trying to lock up the worry and the feelings and move on.

Flashing her new moon tattoo to everyone that would look Joanne is in a polar opposite place, cloud nine with all the hope of a teenager and none of the doubt and angst of a middle-aged raging killer. Catching up with the rest of the group, the show of the tattoo lifts everyone mood, everyone loves a bit of new ink, Indy particularly;

"Wow, far out that's ammmaazzziiing."

As Joanne started to show everyone Dan's new tattoo, the tribute band burst into life, the lyrics could not be more apt, "Gone Wild" the fear of what the 'wild man' has done, Indy already dancing around started dragging everyone towards the band;

"Come on its party time!"

The hours rolled by, the night fueled by whiskey with the group bonded by the journey, a brotherhood and sisterhood of friends, united by the atrocity, that had nearly taken out multiple parts of their group, the darkened valley lit up by the merriment. The stage alive and the band in full flight, raining the guitar fueled rock and roll across the vast audience, partying like nobody else was watching, a freedom in a group, a freedom in large group all non-judgmental, no posers just freedom to express themselves as they choose, people wearing all array of outfits that anywhere else would draw negative sneering looks from the fashion police, who paraded around in a media led judgmental way. Here they could dress as they liked, party as they liked and be who they liked, individualism was the norm! Even Blockhead was surprisingly letting himself go and was in the middle of an air guitar solo completely lost in a world all of his own.

Dancing away, the whole group were individual yet the same, alone yet together, living like tomorrow may never arrive. Joanne looked at her man (she really felt like she had met her man) he was nothing like her normal type, maybe that had always been her problem, the fact she had a type was her problem, the type who just used and abused her, not men of morals and respect;

"My feet are blued from all this walking and we are tattooed, but one thing is still missing yet, take me to the tent and give me the rest."

Dan looked up at the group, who had heard every word and was trying to look like they had not actually heard it, he smiled for the first time that day and wandered off with his maiden. Taking her to her tent to give her what she desired, his feelings different, a melancholy, fuzziness in the back of his head, a relaxed desire to slowly please his new leading lady, an oddness he did not understand and a feeling he was not familiar with, one he tried to push to the side and pretend was not actually there.

The next morning Joanne was up early cooking breakfast from the supplies and camping stove in Blockhead's panniers, her smile and her mood as light as the feeling in her stomach, she opened the tents, allowing the smell of bacon to waft into the them and slowly one by one they all started to appear, apart from Ritchie who for some reason was flat out on his back lying on the grass wearing a nappy and a baby bonnet. As Jack dragged himself from his pit he looked at Ritchie and smiled;

"Oh I do love a rally virgin night"

As Joanne started handing out bacon sandwiches, a security guard rushed past her;

"Jack, Jack you're needed. Now!"

His tone sharp and respectful, with a distinct urgency to it, Jack stood up in just his jeans, still chewing his bacon sandwich, he sauntered off with the security guard. As he reappeared, Jack looked stern, packing up and dressing at once;

"Get your shit together we leave in 10! The police have arrived looking for a man on a bike, who the media are calling the killer biker, needle in a fucking haystack here but the rear gate has just had the lock smashed off, there is a couple of large biker groups who know the full story, who will protect us and act as a cloak to get us out of here, they are about to leave we must be with them and find a way to be lost from this shit! The police are starting to work round the tents with a photograph of you Dan."

CHAPTER 5:

REVELATIONS

The feeling of panic raced around the group. Dan stood rooted to the spot, as still as the trees behind him, Joanne started throwing stuff onto the bike;

"Come on Dan we need to go! Come on we need to ship out, we've got to run for the sun, run for the hills or whatever it is you do, but go!"

The group hurriedly started dismantling the tents and packing, forcing stuff into bags, lashing them down with bungees on to the bikes.

Dan stood both tall and still with a thousand yard stare, looking through the world and seeing no one, then in a deep slow voice spoke;

"Everybody stop! This is the end of the line, I must do this alone it's not your responsibility to look after me, I am a rolling stone and I cannot settle, I cannot stay and you should not be forced to be with me and risk yourselves for me!"

Joanne's face tortured and angry;

"How dare you! You walk into my life smash down my wall of shit and show me another way of life, tease me with excitement then run away. I am coming with you!"

"I am not taking you down with me. I need emancipation, to be a Revelator and to understand my world of shit, to leave my success and failure behind then start again; I can't take you through my pain. I am in a moment of divergence with myself, I can't handle

this and you shouldn't have to, I feel trapped, drowning in guilt and hate for myself for all I have done wrong in my life. I am a failure and a success in equal measure, but today the pain of failure is fresh and new far outweighing my strength to stand"

The sinking in his stomach showed in the pain across his face, as his shoulders dropped and the tears welled in his eyes, it was clear how heavy his life weighed upon him, intensified by the new world of shit he was creating in his cyclical world of terror.

As Indy finished strapping her stuff to the back of her chopper seat, she revealed a side of her no one had ever seen, an anger, a frustration, lost is her care free nature, a new Indy, clearly the last few days had changed her, deeply affecting her whole being;

"What are you running from? What are u scared of? Life? The past? Or the future? All that matters is the moment, the road of life wherever it may lead. You have got to keep up with the moment, not get left behind by your own life. You are the star in your life so play the lead ! If you don't that's the day you die! So pick up your shit and let's go!"

Dan was startled by the sudden change in Indy, fearing he has damaged her gentle caring mind, worrying he had made a negative impact on such a delicate flowering woman. He slowly threw his stuff on the only thing he fully trusted, the one who answered his prayers, listened, provided happiness, forgiveness and retribution given in every twist of the throttle. As he shared a moment with the only constant thing in his life, meaningless metal to some that gives so much happiness and contentment to Dan when coupled with the freedom of the open road, a feeling normally reserved for the protective arm of a father, wrapping around you telling his son that it will be alright.

As the melancholy feeling drifted over him, making his life feel in soft focus, his brow furrowed and his lips tightened. He moved himself towards his bike as a group of black and very loud bikes slowly thundered towards him, big custom shed-built one-off bikes and a few old classics. A custom, fully decked out touring bagger pulled up right next to Jack, leaning it on its butter knife style side stand. The rider dismounted, shaking Jacks hand with the vigour of comradeship;

"You have been a lone wolf too long Jack, I wish I could have tied you down to my chapter, but it's an honour to roll with a brother for who I have so much respect. I guess this is the man for whom the bell now tolls? I have heard some stories about you, and so far you have my respect, however this is a run to the sun, we have some open invites to disappear in to France, travelling down to set up at a rally in Portugal next month, you can come with us but if I feel the need I will run for myself, this is a favour to Jack and should I need to protect my run to the sun, I will leave without you at any point I choose, if you're still with me at the crossing I can get you into France with no passport the rest is up to you, we clear?"

Dan was slightly agitated by being told what to do but nodded his head and straddled his bike, looking at Joanne he gave a half smile knowing he needed to give more, but right now he could barely endure his own emotions. The 'bagger' revved up and the group behind stood their bikes up as if to attention, the first several bikes moving off and creating a gap, allowing Dan and the little group of bikers to slide into the middle. As they trundled along the campsite, the rear group of bikes formed a group around them, shrouding them with a cloak of bikes. Joanne's trepidation stirred and fed her anxiety, but she was developing a *'stand together'* mentality, for richer or poorer and in sickness and in health through the good times and the bad, till death us do part, her emotions awash with fear and a strange excitement, she wanted this man more than she wanted anything.

Dan was struggling to hold back a raging sickness in his stomach, a feeling of self-loathing that made his wild head feel heavy and thick, carrying a black cloud around his helmet, the chin piece flicked back over the helmet, leaving the open face of the helmet to show his pain to the world, drawing with him a feeling of being trapped, a burden that he has caused for these good people. If it was not for the fact Joanne was on the back he would pull his shiny black beast out from the pack, fuck them all and come what may, run solo for the hills, rather than take them down with him. The crazed thoughts sharing space in his head with wonderment at the faith of this group;

"Why are these good people sticking by me? Why are they protecting me? Why are they so loyal to someone they hardly know? What have I done to deserve their kindness? How can I ever repay them my gratitude? Can I even bear to accept their kindness?"

The dirt road was bumpy, throwing up dust as they sneaked out of a small little known gateway, passing through fields and rutted ground, not really the normal road Dan found his escape with. The group slowly bounced its way along, all of them wrestled to keep the bikes upright, with Indy struggling the most, her raked out forks bouncing and trembling along, tracking against the direction she wanted to travel, gone was the smile, gone was her hope, gone was her softness.

As they entered the road, various bikes raced to the front, blocking off junctions and traffic allowing the group to never slow down, creating a sense of control, having the audacity not to stop for lights and islands, the road was theirs!

"Where were they heading? Where was next? What will happen? What will become of the fun little group he joined?"

Dan's guilt fell onto his mind harder than his fists fell on to the young driver who fell foul to his rage, an anger not entirely for the youth but released from years of hate stored up, hate broken from the 'Pandora's box' that had remained sealed for many years. As they rolled onwards, mile after mile, the riders felt the wind cleansing their slightly sweaty, unwashed faces, but not Dan's sins. The scenery changed, from small back roads, heavily tree lined, to wide open A roads. Seeing signs for Nottingham, Dan had a sneaking feeling where they may be spending the night, when they were actually miles from anywhere.

The 'bagger' at the front lifts his hand in the air and waved it in a circle of ceremony, Dan had spent many a night of naughtiness at this place, so many happy times, memories came flooding back into his mind chipping away at his painful sorrow.

As they rode along, an odd entrance looped back on itself, they entered the carpark, there were a number of tents set up and oddly and what looked like the back of a horse sticking out of the hedge. He thought to himself;

"Why would that be there? Why not I suppose?"

The mood of the 1% er group stirred in the atmosphere of rolling burn outs, wheelies and revving engines. Another moment of sanctuary in this confused messed up world, a place where you could be who or what you want, surely the real utopian dream to be who you are not who you're expected to be?

The 'bagger' drew his chapter together and led them away, parting with;

"You guys grab some of those blue tents; they are yours for the night."

Leaving them, he leads his chapter inside. The ride had lifted the mood of the group like only a ride could, giving an upbeat and happy go lucky feeling, a sense of hope and freedom, smiles all around. Richie has his speakers set up and already playing, blasting out some old school rock he knew the group would like. Drums beating and wrestling with a bass guitar truly lifting everyone, everyone but Dan. He was still sombre carrying a lead weight around his neck, struggling with the risk he has put upon the group;

"Listen everyone your all such amazing people and you have stood by me, but this has to be the end of the road, I can't risk affecting your lives with myworld of shit I have created, I have messed up again and I am done, this has to be the last night you guys risk yourselves for me. I am going to get some sleep, then first light I will leave with the 1% er's maybe that's where I was destined really anyway."

The group looked on in disbelief with Joanne shaking her head. Blockhead sat casually on his bike looking more alive and content that ever before; he spoke through his teeth like an angry navvy, like a Jack wannabe;

"My life is worthless, rich but worthless, I am full of shit and that shit made me wealthy and I don't give a fuck about my old life, this is my life. I am reborn into this and no way am I giving up now, what's mine is yours, including my new life, with or without you I

am leaving with that bunch of bikers, to get you out of this country. Hell I might even go with you"

Joanne dragged Dan away;

"Come on, what are you doing? You need to stay focused we can leave and start a new life away from the bullshit of our old lives, a drifting vagabond on that beautiful black bike, it would be your ideal life it's you and me!"

Dan hung his head as he hopelessly as he wandered across the field, dragging his old worn boots through the grass, drawing his feelings into the myriad of despair and sorrow, his feelings so mixed and heavy.

"I can't take you with me Joanne"

Her face distorted with pained tears in her eyes, the pain so severe her gut twisted so much she struggled not to 'throw up', her head swirled worse than her stomach, on the edge of happiness she was being discarded, her hopes and dreams slashed, as if with the blade from a Samurai's katana, one swipe had literally cut her in two. Speechless, stunned, slaughtered by the very thought of losing Dan, her leading light, her leading man, her hope, dreams and ambition all rolled into one. After mentally dragging herself from the depth of despair and the torturous words that have tripped off the tortured tongue of her very reason to be;

"No fucking way I would rather stand by you and be slayed by the 4 horsemen of the apocalypse than not be there for you!"

"I am a rolling stone Joanne, I am unwilling to settle a rolling stone gathers no moss, I can't gather any moss I have to move on, I can't stay still I need to taste everything life has to offer and twice if I like it, I will hurt you I always end up hurting someone, I have hurt more people than I can remember, I am a bad egg a poison! Just

like a rose you may like what you see, but grab too hard and it will hurt you!"

Joanne was struggling to hold herself together as they stood alone in a field, gazed upon by all, with no one close enough to hear, desperately trying to walk away, rooted to the spot and wanting to scream but her voice was silent, her mixed up crazy contorted mind not allowing any words to come to the front, just a mix of words terrorising her confusing her more. Dan cut her down further as his onslaught of samurai slashes start to really bite at her.

"I am not taking you down with me you deserve better than this, I want emancipation and to be a revelator, cleaning out my life and starting a fresh, leaving behind all my success and failures"

His words had taken her wildly beating heart and strangled it, crushed her desire and love of life. She'd been raised from the depths of boredom to the happiness of a carefree life, to be distraught and battered by a brutal slaying of one man. Slowly she drew all her strength, gathering her self-respect and her emotions together she prepared for her first blow back at Dan, with a desire to hurt him, expose him, make him feel a small amount of what she has just experienced. He was not an easy man to attack, far too guarded and strong with his locked up set of emotions, hidden away from sight, buried deep in his inner core.

"What is it with you? As soon as we get somewhere you want an easy way out of the mess you created, you're a pussy! You're scared! What are you scared of little boy? Is it yourself? Love? Who damaged you and why are you so fucked up? You're not the man I thought you were! You're weak, a child of a man on the run! What are you scared of?"

The anger and hurt strewn across her face as she glared deep into Dan's eyes, her rage matching that of Dan's and her nose wrinkled as she scowled at a man she'd thought was everything, who now threatened to cast her aside and leave her swirling in a dusty car park surrounded by people and yet alone. Dan looked at his once fair maiden who now looked hurt, abused and low. Dropping his gaze to his old scuffed boots, avoiding the ever present pain in her face;

"All that matters is the moment, the road of life wherever it may lead. I have got to keep up with the moment not get left behind by my own life. As Indy said; I am the star in my life so I will play the lead, if I don't that's the day I die!"

Joanne's horror and disbelief weighed her emotions down, causing a feeling of despair to slowly engulf her, a black cloud slowly descended around her, slipping down her neck and around her shoulder til it reached her stomach, where it wrapped ever tighter around her waist slowly choking her entire being.

The group awkwardly shuffled into the tents, leaving Dan and Joanne to it. They discussed what would happen if Dan left alone, what should they do? Maybe onwards with the 1% ers? They all started to unpack and once again with a feeling of uncertainty threw their stuff in tents, not sure what the new day would bring, creating a feeling of vagueness and ambiguity, leaving them all with a sinking ship of sorrow not the happy go lucky feeling they expected to be enjoying.

Dan walked slowly over to a bench next to the green bushy and unkempt hedgerow, sitting with his head slightly consumed by the leafy line of protection, cloaking his shoulders, as if trying to become part of the bush itself.

"Joanne you have to understand."

His voice croaked and stumbled like a teenager breaking his voice, the pain of what he was about to say leaving him cold and hard faced, digging up memories he had long tried to forget.

"My crown of shit is exactly that, I am a mixed-up teenager in a man's body dealing with adulthood badly"

Dan explained how at the age of 13 his dad had shot his mum in a drunken rage over some bullshit his dad thought was important. He had abused them both for years before. As his mother lay there with the bullet lodged in her chest, her arm reached out towards him, with her face screwed up in pain she'd told Dan to run and make his own life without them. The words were still tripping off her fresh blood red tongue when his dad fired the WW2 pistol, firing a bullet straight into her head, then looking a young helpless Dan in the eye, he placed the gun in his own mouth, starting to cry before he pulled the trigger.

It was the worst noise Dan had ever heard as his dad's body fell against the corpse of his mother. That moment had ripped Dan's heart in two, the blackness of evil replacing the aspirations and desires that had previously ran through the hopeful youth, the zest for life draining out across the floorboards, staining the rug, his mother and father lying dead in front of him. The imprint of this moment constantly stabbed at Dan mentally shaping who he became and who he would always be, socially stratified by a moment out of his control.

Joanne's hands were clasped tightly over her mouth with tears streaming down her face; no noise just the horror of imagining the scene, a young innocent boy torn apart by the actions of a deranged father;

"Dan I can't imagine how? Why? What? I actually don't know what to say!"

Dan's mean and moody protective shield was in full flight, a stern angry grimace of a face repressing the dark dank memories of a childhood erased in early teenage confusion. On that day Dan's anger was born and anger that had haunted him all his life, no vent, no outlet and certainly no support.

"I lived in the shed for a few weeks watching the police come and go, until I was caught stealing food from my neighbours. Gathering together what I needed to survive, I said a little thank you to myself every time I took some food. I hated stealing but needed to survive, Morris and Dotty were so kind to me, they took me in and raised me as their own, we never discussed what I had done or why they took me in, they just got on with life as if I was their son, the old fashioned way stiff upper lip and carry on regardless! They were good to me they gave me what I needed and more besides, the happiest part of my life was spending time with Morris in his shed, working on his motorbike, with his wife Dotty brining us tea (enough tea to sink a ship) and huge slices of cake"

Dan talked so harshly, as if telling a story of anger not one of happy times, but the bad outweighed the good, the memory of his dead mother with his dad slumped across her was the memory of family he carried in his head, overpowering the happy family memories of Morris and Dotty.

Joanne placed a hand on his shoulder;

"Are you okay? What happened to Morris and Dotty, are they still alive?"

The words struck Dan harder that she imagined his face contorted, red eyes bulging, he swallowed hard fighting his tears, burying his emotions and beating them back like a fire. His distorted face was unable to stop the tears rolling down his cheek, rippling across the lines in his skin;

"When I was about 23 they were robbed and Dotty confronted them with her coal shovel and was beaten to death by the thief with her own shovel"

He could no longer hold it together, his heart literally pouring its hurt out onto his face, screwing his face up he explained he got the call whilst he was working away, by the time I got home the police were there they had arrested thief who was now in custody. Morris was distraught, his childhood sweetheart taken from him while he was fetching her fresh baking ingredients, flowers and her favourite chocolates.

"We consoled each other sobbing from the pits of our stomachs the entire night, we didn't leave the house or each other's side till the day of her funeral, the days passed slowly, scaring each of us as neither of us were prepared to discuss our feelings, typical men not wanting any help, storing all the grief and issues, packing them away, no words were spoken just sorrow and grief etching its way in to our souls, chewing away at our life and destroying our inner spark".

Dan looked awful and was clearly reliving it as if it was fresh;

"The funeral was as Dotty requested in her will; small and simple, she didn't like money wasted on fancy nothings as she called them. Both of us were dressed in black suits, white shirts and pain written across our faces, standing at her grave silently like we needed to, with others' patting us on the back and giving condolences. They were doing what they thought was right. But I had a rage, a rage of revenge the need to avenge her death to shed my pain to another, I had a desire to destroy a life, stronger than life itself, I battled with it, pushed it to one side, but it kept picking at me, biting at me and winding me up. On the outside I stood a man grief stricken, on the inside I stood a man of war hotter than the Devils fork, with more rage than any one heart can hold, even one as black as mine!"

After the funeral and still in his black suit Morris packed his sidecar which was bolted to his old 50's classic motorbike, that Dan and Morris had rebuilt it in his shed over many years, they both knew every nut, bolt and weld on that bike spending many happy hours rebuilding and customising the engine and putting in to the frame, it was to be better than any Isle of man bike of its day, they regularly joked about racing it in the classic races on the Isle of Man.

"Morris left me at this point he was still barely able to speak or deal with the fact that his happiness, his love, his reason for everything was gone, he forced out a few mumbled words he said he was going to clear his head and when it's clear he will return; that was nearly 30 years ago! Last I heard he was living off the grid in Europe".

Joanne's face was still in horror of the atrocity she had imagined, the feelings Dan must have had, and was still so obviously carrying on his back today, dragging him down. She managed to pull herself together bushing away her own tears and asked Dan;

"How did you deal with that?"

The pain of the answer was clear in Dan's eyes as he squinted a sideways look at her;

"Do you want the truth?"

Her reply was an obvious one;

"Always".

"The guy who killed Dotty was let go after 6 months in prison due to him having some kind of diminished responsibility, arguing

she attacked him whilst he was in her kitchen and he defended himself but went too far"

Dan turned away screwing his face to the side stifling the emotions dragging them deep inside like he always did, he explained he struggled with work, with life, with drink and drugs, until the release date of Dotty's murderer was printed in the local news, on this day the world changed forever as the report mentioned that Dotty's killer only had weeks left to serve in prison.

With a clear mind and having not drank in weeks, Dan had known which prison her killer had bent sent to and what date he would be released. Information from the press was plentiful; they had created a media frenzy over the ordeal, printing the details including the guy's name and a picture of him. When Dan had read Billy, Dotty's murderer, would be released in a few weeks' time, he started his project of darkness.

Dan had already bought a cheap old 90's four cylinder Japanese bike to make a large 1200 café racer from, fitted with a loud exhaust to start with, he now customised it for one purpose, pain. In the shed he adapted the bike with many homemade features, things that should not be done too bikes. His deathly modifications included a padlock with a special chain, coiled onto a roller bearing down the side of the engine. The bike was very much a rat bike, resembling something from 'Mad Max' with rushed welds and parts that did not belong. He had attached to the bike a flame thrower, situated between the speedo and rev counter, which he connected to a fuel line, finally he fitted a spiked tyre that would normally be used on ice.

Dan had sat for hours on the bike, his instrument of death, at the end of the prison road, waiting and agonising over the death of Dotty. The tears rolling down his face, soaking into his beard making it slightly damp, she was the only person who had truly had his back, who actually really cared for him and showed it daily. As Dan waited, the rage terrorised his mind, twisting him inside out making him angry at the world, he saw the Devil himself walk out the gates, both 'cocky' and smiling as if he had won. Dan was ripped in two by a righteous rage, his hands actually hurting with how tight he was gripping the bars of his bike, eyes wider than the sun, equally burning as bright and as hot. Dan had no cause or consequence in his frantic mind, just revenge and hurt fuelling him.

As the laughing prisoner took off and turned the corner Dan started his shed built weapon, the 4 cylinder old school carburettor engine spitting flames from the short stubby exhaust as Dan blipped the throttle. He opened the throttle wide open and the spikes on the ice tyre ripped into the grooves of the tarmac, gripping then slipping, lifting the front wheel and kicking the rear sideways, lurching the bike forwards and sideways like a bucking bronco. Dan was not aware of the danger, he had no fear, he had no emotion at all he was null, muted and purposeful like a machine about to complete an order.

As Dan turned the corner the rear wheel slid violently sideways, the bike struggling for grip on its spiked rear tyre, he wrestled the bike upright. With an upward lunge the bike kicked around between his legs; the prisoner turned in shock looking at the sight flying towards him dressed in black leather with a black helmet and a black visor. Looking like one of the four horsemen of the apocalypse and bringing with him the evils that would only come at the end of the world.

The bike was aimed straight at Billy, who was rooted with fear to the ground, unable to move let alone run. He was a coward who had sought out vulnerable people to rob, he was a parasite a blood sucker, an oxygen thief who did not deserve a life. As the bike approached Billy, Dan grabbed the padlock ripping the chain from its holder, causing the crudely attached roller bearing to spin loudly as the chain unravelled from it, causing sparks as it was released from its hiding place, Dan flung the chain outwards, whipping it straight across the fear stricken, weak man who stood before him, smashing the chain into his chest. As it dug into his flesh the end of the chain whipped around him thumping him in the back, the chain had been sharpened to make the links pointed, as Dan rode past, the links ripped at Billy's chest spinning him around like a child's spinning top throwing him against the wall. Billy was slowly sliding down the wall gasping for breath dazed, confused and pained.

Dan was not finished; he wanted Billy to suffer for the rest of his life. Billy was now lay on the floor facing upwards with the midday sun beating down on his face, he was breathing heavily with his body in shock, his mind spinning wildly giving him fight and flight but neither could lift him from his beaten state. As he lay on the pavement with a ring of blood weeping from his chest, piercing his now ripped white tee shirt. Throwing the chain on the ground, Dan rode the bike up on to the pavement, he locked the rear wheel skidding it towards Billy, he released the rear brake and rolled both wheels over his arm, the spikes of the rear wheel piercing the skin as they rolled over it.

Listening to Billy scream filled Dan with a psychopathic delight, a slight smile at each corner of his mouth covered by the black helmet. He backed the rear tyre up against the side of Billy's chest looking like he was parking the bike between his torso and arm, the engine was so loud it was deafening Billy, the exhaust above his head bellowing out the war cry of a 4 cylinder rage that Dan possessed. As Billy lay bleeding and broken on the floor, Dan locked the front brake and did a 'burn out' against Billy, the spikes ripping at his torso and his arm, pulling flesh and muscle off both, each spike ripping deeper till they scored the bone. Dan let go of the front brake allowing the bike to speed off, bouncing down the kerb, turning the bike around he aimed the flamethrower at a man already delirious with pain, unable to cope with the torture he was enduring, Dan was not finished yet. He wanted to leave this man scarred and hurt just like Dotty had been at the end of her life.

The lack of emotion Dan felt at this point left him in a psychopathic, militant state, a robot completing a mission. He faced the bike at the man who had destroyed his new rebirth of life, his second chance of a family. Dan lifted his black visor and with a stern face and a thousand yard stare he pulled the trigger on the flame thrower igniting more pain, allowing him to burn, the smell of charring and melting flesh filled Dan's nostrils, but he did not flinch, he did not show any emotion, just completed the task, void of any emotion.

Billy lay on the floor screaming, barely able to move, as Dan started unclicking the modifications and tossing them in his bag, he pulled out a mini fire extinguisher and put the tortured oxygen thief out. He lay motionless but alive, just as planned so he could live out his life painfully physically and mentally scarred just as Dan was. Seeing him lying tortured and pained on the floor brought the feeling back to Dan. He had feelings again, that he hadn't felt many things but at least he felt, he felt alive. The final part of Dan's plan to be executed for his premediated shed built weapon of war, was now to disconnect the fuel line that was extended for the flame thrower and aim it down at the engine. As the petrol poured onto the red hot exhaust the bike burst into flames, Dan let go of the bike and allowed in to fall on the floor, as it engulfed itself in a protective flame of hidden delight, his alibi was to be of an argument and a crash that did the damage to Billy.

Joanne was dumbstruck, her mind unable to comprehend the evil Dan had shown. He looked at her struggling with the past pain and the new pain that came from the disappointment in her face, Dan's head was as low as his voice when he let out a gruff speech;

"Evil has been a friend of mine, I have been dark all my life and that's why I cherish the good, the sweet and loyal, respect brings out my softness and my care, a lack of respect brings out the dark from within me!"

Dan had done his time and paid his penance in Wakefield prison. He served 7 years of a 13 year sentence, for a crime that had left a man barely alive, with vengeance burned all over him, leaving Dan with a criminal record for attempted murder. Dan's plan to be acquitted had failed. However, the revenge and closure had been worth the jail time to Dan, he felt alive again but it had cost him his freedom. He needed to hurt him as much as the hurt he'd felt;

"Joanne please don't hate me I know I am a beast, I am evil, but I am also a good caring man, I needed closure yes I did hurt him just to see his pain, I have no shame, a man's got to do what a man's got

to do! I know I did wrong, I lost a lot but I gained too. I offloaded some of my pain to someone who stole my happiness; the torture was worth it to just to avenge Dotty's death"

She could see the crazy, mixed-up emotion weighing him down, not sure he was actually right about offloading his pain, as he looked in great pain right now, she put a hand on his knee, looked into his eyes, they were empty as if a light had been turned out;

"Dan I am in love with you, I am part of you I want to take our lives on as one, and together united we are stronger to face anything! What do you want?

Dan's reply of emancipation to be set free from the legal social and political world, to be liberated from this awful collapsing society, would have been enough to stop her heart dead, but she now she understood his journey, his reason and his way. She had one question in her mind and one alone;

"Dan do you not yearn to love and be loved?"

CHAPTER 6:

DESIRES

Dan's pain was still contorting his heavily lined face, one eye half closed with pain in his mind, as he spoke from his heart;

"I do want to, I do have desire and love, I do want happiness but my cold black heart coupled with my thick hardened mind makes it hard"

His words fell upon Joanne's ears nicely as she saw a broken man, a man who she could help rebuild and join as one true love, a man who yearned for the love he never had. In truth it was the love he vaguely remembered from his childhood and that he had once tasted the sweetness of with Dotty, the closest he had ever felt to anyone.

Dan muttered out from underneath his heavy breath;

"I hang my head in shame as my heart cries in disgrace for my soul, but I had to do it or the pain would have consumed me and destroyed me, the pain I am left with lets me know I am alive, but to turn it to joy I need a three figure heart beat and enough adrenaline to sink a ship."

His weary soulless voice droned on;

"I have a joy of solitude with a few choice people I can trust, I don't really feel anything unless I am experiencing it at 100%, anything less than that and the feeling is weak, often not felt at all, if it is not full flavour, full fat or maximum impact, anything normal for me and I feel nothing, it barely scratches passed my hardened black

heart. If I am not at that three-figure heart beat I feel nothing, I am just dead, emotionless, painless and just waiting, waiting for the next moment that can fill my need for 100% desire, 99% is not enough, it's all or nothing for me."

As the pair sat in silence Joanne's head tilted to one side as she considered where he had been, the torture he'd endured, the pain he'd hidden, how has this man had not fallen apart like his father did or was Dan just running from his past, outrunning his density, trying not to become his father?

"Dan I love you and hope deep down you love me too, I will be by your side, but you need to let me stand beside you! It's not where you are coming from that is important but where you are going? Where are you going?"

"Any fucking where WE like!"

The words lifted her skyward as it was the first time she felt she had actually broken into the damaged broken heart of Dan, the first time he'd allowed her in, the first time she felt this might actually go somewhere long term, as she thought to herself;

"He said we not I"

Dan had a small twitch in his eye as the pain still bit at him , as he explained his fear of society, the 'broken society', the reason why he reacted so badly to the drunken texting driver, he couldn't stand the disrespectful, self-entitled, take from society type who only cared about themselves and nobody else!

Dan's explanation of society was so damning of humankind, the 'nirvana' he dreamed of did not exist in this decaying world, but his world within it needed watering and tending to allow it to grow, a place of sanctuary set up to feed his happiness and allow him to recharge from the constant rotting society, in which the sheeple spiral within and cyclically repeating the same behaviour, hoping they get different results. Well one plus one is two till something changes, change the inputs and the outputs will be different, but change the wrong input and the same result still happens, one times one is still one, but two times one is a different result, it often took many attempts to find the right inputs and that why many would never find the utopian results we all crave.

The cloud in people's heads, causing depression and making them to spin out of control, creating an anxiety caused by the herded life they live, never stepping out of the cycle, not changing the inputs, but feeling like everyone else has it better than them, the media image portrayed by their so called friends feeding the spiral of anxiety that is constantly dragging them down, creating a dark cloud that was slowly descending upon and covering any creativity and hope, till people just accepted their own hum drum lives and the never ending cycle of hope destined to be shattered into broken shards of despair!

The combination of those two thoughts, coupled with his past torture is what had consumed both Dan and Joanne, but this moment of hope showed that the cloak of darkness could lift. They had an opportunity to rise and create *'their world'* within the real world, a little place of sanctuary where only happiness could roam free. All were born free with hope creativity and dreams, but became corrupted by society.

Dan broke the silence with a defiant statement that stirred them both up, to rise from the pit in which they sat;

"I was free like the wild wind, like a raging river and like the birds flying high in the sky, I need to move on like that rolling stone, clean out my life, the good and the bad, I need to let that cloak of

darkness fall from my shoulders to the ground, dragging with it my empty void and blackened heart. Only what I can carry on my bike is actually needed!"

Joanne's hope crept slowly across her face, from a small grin in one corner of her mouth and a lifted eyebrow, the pain in her mind slowly flowing away and the sickness in her stomach settled;

"Do I still fit on that bike of yours?"

Dan's smile was strong, his head still low but his eyes fixed on hers, the shared moment joyous, her heart fluttered with the birds, his heart beat like a bass guitar, both were lifted, feeling optimism and joy. Joanne needed Dan and Dan needed her, they both had something to give each other and the need for each other was even stronger than the bike they rode in on.

Dan struggled to allow the feeling, still grimacing and controlling his smile, Joanne couldn't hide her feelings, they were written all over her face. The feeling of the freedom in a broken world was empowering as Dan told her;

"All I need is you and my bike"

The words lit her up brighter than a lighthouse on a stormy night, the warm feeling flooding through her body, her hope gaining momentum;

"So what do you propose Mr whatever I can get? Where do we go in this fucked up world?"

Dan's pained face was now more quizzical and his reply even more confusing;

"I don't know, where is left?"

The words felt hollow and were as if there were just hanging in the air, swirling around in their heads, as Dan shifted in his seat from a slumped downtrodden look to a bolt upright position demonstrating an air of power and strength, his face stern and his lips tight, a raging inferno building in the pit of his stomach as he contemplated the broken world.

Dan started a speech like a leader rallying his troops;

"The world is becoming feral, dark and evil, people only having one purpose, to be better than the next person, even if they have to stand on them to get higher, people literally only want more wealth, status, power or validation so they feel better than anyone else. That's why the super fake people are all over TV, people want to emulate them for money, power and status! Civilisation as we know it ended over a decade ago, the greedy self-entitled 'want it all now' type are taking over! We are one step away from a dystopian baron wasteland where small groups steal and kill to get what they want, fighting over diminishing resources, we are heading for that film from the late 70's where a warrior emerges trying to fight against the ever-growing evil gangs, raping and pillaging the world like the old Viking stories. Taking what they want and terrorising the people who won't join them! Where can you hide from it? Where can you keep away from them? Where is left where they won't come for you? The world will be fire, death, torture and 'take, take, take', evil residing over good! Who murdered the world? Who brought us here? Who did this? We did this to ourselves, we allowed it, we didn't stop it, we deserve this vile apocalyptic war of the masses that is on the horizon, we caused it by greed and one-upmanship on our fellow man!"

Joanne's face showed her horror, not fully comprehending what he predicted, not following why or what he has said. Dan launched into his final revelations of his hate of the world.

"I was born free but corrupted by society, free like the wolf roaming around in search of his desires. Redemption is coming and I want to be far away from it, living in my world not everyone else's world! The end of our world is the death of civilisation. All that will remain will be ignorance and self-loathing sprinkled with self-righteousness gratification. We pretend we are gods, when we are insignificant, yet significantly destroying the world we live in and the people who live within it. I fear that the new world will be worse than the old, so I want to drop out and find my own path, like a vagabond I walk alone on this road of despair, searching for that utopian dream of no past, no future, just the now, me in the moment, no place to be, just living as I please, when I please, how I please, away from the sheeple who are herded through life controlled by media, education and the worry they might be different from one another. Well I am different and I am proud of it. I want to be different; I want different things for different reasons, that is the way of Dan, that is the way of true happiness. True love and respect is the song I sing and I resent the masses and their ways of anxiety and self-promotion! I travel in my direction regardless of theirs."

The words shook Joanne, stirring and whirling around her, they gave her a mixed up confused cerebral melee, which spun her mind vigorously into a state of contrasting arguments, raging against each other in her own head, as she gathered together her conflicting thoughts, she uttered a phrase;

"Was it Mark Twain who said 'When you find yourself on the side of the masses it's time to pause and reflect'? I have always liked the notion that I should be the black sheep and be different from people, I was always told I was a weird kid"

As Dan raised his head, he allowed the smugness to ripple across his face, forcing his shoulders back and puffing out his chest. Dan explained to Joanne;

"You are the black sheep, the weird child and that's what makes you special, you should wear that as a badge of honour on a crown, being considered crazy or different is a compliment when it comes from the victims of cultural conditioning, people fear the different, as it shows them what they could do if they dared, but they don't dare for the fear of the vulture masses ridiculing them for not looking or acting the same as them. Who should say what looks good and be right, it's only their opinion and opinions are like arseholes, every fucker's got one! The masses walk the well-trodden line of the cattle, blindly following for following sake, fearing standing out or being different just to be controlled and kept in line!"

Joanne laughed as she replied;

"You always wear black, black shirt, black jacket, black trousers, black boots and even a black bike!"

The words made Dan visibly uncomfortable as he shifted from side to side, losing the smug look on his face and staring down at his black scruffy boots and his black scruffy jeans, but as ever the confident look in his face was never far away, destroying the kicked feeling he had from the words from the only person who could talk to him like this, without a rampaging bull response;

"You see a wise man once said I wear black to remind me that I am not special, and for all the darkened troubled souls in the world, I wear black as it matches my mood, my soul and my heart"

The effect of Dan was clearly rubbing off on Joanne as she developed a smug retort with a look that said, 'I will cut you down to size';

"Maybe one day Dan someone will lift your blackened heart and you will not need to dress in black!"

Dan's rollercoaster of emotions churned in his stomach making him feel queasy, as the emotions swallowed the colour from his face and pulled his lips tight;

"I feel like a revelator asking my own questions and finding my own answers the revelations are not always right, but they develop into the surprise I had first searched for, Joanne what do you search for? What is your utopia?"

The moment hung in the air, floating unopened and untouched with the wind gently blowing Joanne's hair across her face, she was in full thought, full of confusion and in full flight with her mixed-up new desires;

"My utopia is to be free, to feel the wind in my face and the sun on my back, to develop a free love where the sun shines in my mind every day, cuddled up in my life with no dramas just peace and solitude. I want you Dan that's what I want. I see us growing old, you tinkering with whatever you need in a shed and me bringing you cups of tea, having horses, chickens and goats, but you have shown me excitement like I have never had before, you have awakened me to the thrill of danger and the thrill of passion, I am more alive than I have ever been and that's down to you. I love the danger of us running from the police, I love the risks, I love the speed, noise and vibrations of the bike, I love you!"

Those words equally excited and scared Dan, the face of a scared man looked back at her, the usual face a man pulled when those three words bounced off the ear drums unexpectedly, the surprise in his face was slowly subsiding south as his chin dropped and his mouth opened. The silence was deafening, the inability for Dan to return the words weighed down on him, crushing his spine under the weight of the three tiny words;

"I... um yeah, you see I find... um... yeah"

She slowly held out a slender finger laying it gently on his lips, she reassured him, telling him;

"You don't need to say it, until you can say it and mean it, I just thought you should know why I am still here and why I won't leave you."

Out of the eerie light creeping over the hedgerow a figure appeared like an angel stood in the half light, Jack stood in front of them seeming taller than ever, with two new badges stitched on to his cut, they read 'Master At Arms'. He was not one to gloat or to show his excitement, but his stance spoke for him as he stood with his chest puffed out and his shoulders back, his chin higher than ever, he looked like he owned the world.

"Are you two lovebirds still out here? You need to pack up we are leaving in two hours there is food inside so fill your boots it's going to be a long day."

Joanne looked deeply at Jack seeing how happy he looked and asked;

"What is Master at Arms?"

The reply was short, sharp and to the point with an odd smile creeping out the side of his stern lips;

"The judge, the jury, and the hangman. That's what."

With that he headed off, shaking each one of the tents, waking everybody up;

"Those who ride with us get up. Those that do not, disappear. You were never here!"

His words hanging in the air, Jack strode off in a quick march back to the main building.

Slowly the group climbed out of the tents, a buzz of noise starting to unfold and a new dawn leading their hope. Blockhead is up and out first, emulating Jack, following his stride and desperate to impress his new unlikely hero. Emily and Benjie shared a look that only a couple who had spent so many years together could have. A look of understanding, knowing what the other was thinking. Benjie winked at his sweetheart and he replied to her before she could even ask the question;

"He sure is Jack's new best friend"

Jack stood a much bigger man than his size. A giant of a man in attitude. His voice deep and low, almost inaudible, but the gravel voice intensified, sending a shiver down everyone's back, his ability to strike fear and control a room of people was ever present. His expressions spoke for him, as he guided people to play their little part in his quest. Like a puppet master he oversaw the room, controlling them with his manner and gestures, however when he spoke time stood still. Everybody listened as his words chilled them to the bone;

"Blood is red, till it dries a shade of black, it's thicker than any water and we are all family now as blood has been jointly shed. Most don't realise that when people quote blood is thicker than water, it means the bloodshed in battle bonds men together more than the amniotic fluid of family, you cannot force someone to respect you, but you can choose to not be disrespected, the blood maybe blackened but that's our bond, your families will not fight for you like a man who has shed blood with you. Again, blood is thicker than water, black it may be but that's our colours! We stay together, nobody left behind we are one, we eat as one and we sleep as one. We die as one!"

The group were left stunned as Jack stuffed a huge bap of bacon and sausage into his mouth with egg running down his forearm. He looked like a modern day Viking, gorging before he rampaged across the country.

He roared;

"Eat!"

The group all began to shuffle food on to paper plates, the food of champions, the food of war, hearty, meaty and greasy. Dan grabbed at the food filling his plate with greasy bacon, sausage, two eggs and a wad of bread, then he gently placed a neat plate full of bacon and egg layered on a slice of bread, before turning and handing it to Joanne. His care for her was obvious, more obvious than he realised. Benjie did similar, preparing him and his wife a good breakfast. As he walked over to her carrying their breakfast the mental connection is brighter than the early morning sun, Joanne couldn't help but smile, she wanted what they had and today was maybe the start of it. Richie was unable to hide his youth as he filled his plate and his mouth as fast as he could, loving the free meal. The rest continue eating apart from Indy who was picking her way around looking for whatever took her fancy. She has no idea what she wanted and she liked it that way, floating around not really sure but putting a piece of bacon in a bread roll and nibbling delicately on it just like the young free spirited lady she was.

The war cry of the 1% er spluttered into life, more than a dozen old V twins, vibrating and assaulting the fresh peaceful air from outside. Jack got off his bike slowly, gazing around it, as if adoring it longingly, it was the closest Jack had ever got to love, reaching down to the front cylinder wall of his vibrating push rod old school v twin, he gently felt the air-cooled love affair, checking its warmth, he moved his hand to the rear cylinder with the care one would give a baby, he moved his hands to the top of the engine, feeling the valves vibrate in the heads, allowing the warmth to transfer to his hands, telling him it was ready to roar. He grabbed the throttle, as he revved it hard, the band of men behind him echoed him, revving their engines, literally shaking the ground, howling to the pack of wolves, come join us, the pride in Jack filling him, almost exploding inside him, making him feel complete, he had gravitated to what he needed, he was at one as the excitement and adrenaline flooded around him, lifting his head in to the clouds. The noise was drawing everyone together with a nervous excitement, non-more so than Joanne, lost somewhere in her journey but with a faith she was going in the right direction.

Joanne climbed aboard the bike, the dirty black beast used but never tired, as Dan fired it up the bike shook its huge engine violently. Overcome with nerves that made her hands tremble, a single bead of sweat ran down her spine. As it reached the crack of her bum a faint chill rolled down her back too, her left leg twitched as she sat upon the throttle twisting titan of a bike. Her heart was beating so fast in her chest, almost leaving her breathless. Dan pursed his lips, squinting his eyes like an old cowboy about to ride a after a bull, the trepidation of his journey coupled with his mixed-up memories and feelings of the past, with his overbearing hate for the new world, drawing a sickness is his stomach, his nose wrinkled as he swallowed the vomit burning his throat that had crept in to his mouth. He knew this was the start of everything or the end of everything, this actually could be his last day of his life or the first day of a new life. He quenched his feeling with a rage in his head shouting 'rock and roll mother fucker!'

The pack follows Blockhead from the breakfast, hurriedly jumping on their bikes, not wanting to be left behind. Indy's 70's chopper sat shaking away as if holding back before it leapt into action, Richie revved his super moto, but it was drowned out by the mass of bigger engines, he is not fazed, the youthful hope driving him through not caring about consequence, just right there in that moment and loving it. Good old Benjie and Emily did not care what people thought, they were not trying to impress or intimidate anybody, just Benjie leaning back rubbing his wife's leg as they sat on his old classic parallel twin, reassuring her he knew she was scared as he whispered;

"I got you babe. Always have, always will"

The moment of love and security silenced all around them, as they were lost in their own little world, where nothing but the two of them existed. Blockhead climbed aboard his dealership queen bike, as he looked down he does need a more fitting bike this one is far too bling, but for now I am the dealership queen, but that will change.

Jack slowly rode his bike down the long drive way to the road, turning the hairpin bend steady and sure. As he approached the road he raised his hand and signalled to the front and with one swift motion two bikes rampaged to the front, blocking the road. Jack led the group out without even checking the road for traffic, knowing that his guys had his back, his blockers were stopping the traffic with the shining, chromed war horses and with the menacing 'fuck you' look that all can see in their open face helmets .The chapter president rode behind Jack, also in an open face helmet with an expression on his face that would turn most to stone.

As they all set out on to the road a 4x4 with tinted windows was parked in the field at the end of the driveway, a lone woman wearing a baseball cap and jacket with a high collar, was slumped into the driver's seat, staring intently, watching them leave. As the blockers re-joined the back of the pack two more riders raced to the front to block the traffic lights. Although the lights are red the group rode through the blocked off junction, poetry in motion, no rush just the rapid out runners rotating the job of blocking the junctions and traffic lights. As the back of the group rolled through the lights, the 4x4 started and cautiously began to follow, keeping her distance from the trundling pack of bikes with crazed out runners blocking every junction.

As Jack led his majestic run of warriors, his thoughts turned to his new job, the one he should have taken several years ago before he went lone from his pack, his route is meticulously planned to the rally in Portugal, each bike but the front two packed with a bag of drugs to sell, he is back in the world he had stepped out of, but it gave him an excitement he could not explain, a wave of danger and pride all rolled into one, this was the life he should never have turned his back on, the raging exhilaration stirring in his body, wave after wave of joy, with the sun shining on his face and wind rushing past him, left him in a trance of internal combustion and wind in the face.

As the group rolled on, edging closer to the crossing, the danger will rise and so will the excitement, Jack was torn between his new brothers and his old, but Jack's old brothers needed leading to the sea crossing and organising in the timeslot where they wouldn't be checked. As they moved on to the motorway the group regathered to a close riding pack of bikes, exciting some on the road in a movement of noise, scaring some as they passed by but serving as an annoyance to most as they weave through the mundane boxes of no lifers, just going through life with no excitement, work, eat, sleep, repeat till the day they die in their dull, boring life.

The 4x4 was easily able to track behind the group on the motorway, keeping its distance, the lone woman carried her pain on her back, fantasising about just driving straight at them all and ploughing through them, but the risk she might not get away from them afterwards kept her in check. But the resentment that tarnished her heart stirred a hatred, only feelings of revenge can create. She weaved from lane to lane, holding back a few hundred meters in the hope to not be noticed, no plan, just the fuel of revenge and hate burning her up inside.

Jack's careful plans brought them to leave the motorway, heading to a little petrol station in Evesham on the way to some amazing roads he knew, down through the beauty of the English countryside, heading for the crossing from Poole to Cherbourg in a velvet coated green cloak of trees and countryside and not much else, the perfect run to the sun escape route. Rolling into the petrol station a helicopter circled above as they all filled the tanks on their bikes before the last run to the border.

Jack walked in with a bag full of money, people stood aside and started to whisper behind him, Jack did not even register them in his mind, as he dropped a huge wad of cash on the counter and looked stern. The young geeky guy stuttered;

"Aaaare you the r..r...road executer?"

"The fucking who? I am the man your daddy warned you about, now how much do we owe?"

As the young guy starts counting the cash, Jack stared at the newspapers on the side of the counter, a picture of Dan holding the phone and the vodka from the dead boy, the headline read 'Vengeful Angel' the sub-heading told of a biker executing the filth from the road, drunk drivers and 'texters' beware he is after you! The boy puts the cash in the till;

"You guys are heroes; the media has gone wild for you. All over social media, people are saying you are going to rid the roads of 'scum' people are tracking you wanting to join you ride with you join your cause, you are famous bro."

"I am not your fucking bro you cuntybollocks, are we done?"

Jack strode out bigger than ever, unsure of his next move, 'Tell them all or hide it? Fuck it lets ride!' And with that he gathered them all together, motioned for the out runners and led the pack out on to the road, a whirl of dust kicking up from all the wheels as they left, a merriment from all as they rode on, full of fuel, bikes revving to the limiter, rolling burn outs and horns blasting. The young guy in the petrol station filmed them leaving live on his phone, live onto social media, the likes and comments flooding in as it is shared far and wide in a matter of minutes, with a media frenzy all over it: #roadexecuter #vengefullangel, as the dust settled on the petrol station, the guy behind the counter drifted off into a hazy daydream, wishing he could be part of them as he thought to himself, 'I need a bike that's what I need.'

His dreams were short lived as a suited man walked in, flashing his police badge and demanding the footage from the CCTV, as the woman in the 4x4 followed him in. Paying for her stuff she opened her purse, the picture of her and a badly burnt man flicking into view as she took out her money, the tears well in her eyes as she looks at her man so badly scarred, her love for him blinding her to his disfigurement but enraging her about Dan, she threw the money on the side and hurries back to her 4x4, a uniformed officer reaches out asking

"Are you okay Miss?"

The anger woven into her face communicates more to the police officer than words ever could she mutters:

"I will be!"

Slamming her car door she drove straight over the bin at the end of the pump leaving a scratch the length of the car, the graze to her 4x4 and the police watching her did not even touch her stony exterior, not even getting close to affecting her, she was a woman with revenge on her mind, bitter and twisted up inside, wanting to give as much pain as she was able to, wanting to stamp over anybody who got in her way, the woman reached across into her glove box pulling out a small revolver with a very detailed embossed finish, ornate pretty and deadly, just like her!

CHAPTER 7:

RUN FOR YOUR LIFE

Jack led the pack with all the other bikes following behind him, his lips stern and his eyes squinted behind his sunglasses, mean, moody and melancholy all rolled in to one, the thought of what the petrol station guy said still buzzing around his head, forging mixed emotions. He worried about too much media attention as it could really fuck up his whole agenda!

As the bikes thundered through the lush countryside in the vale of the secluded countryside and the swooping valleys, it was a young lover's paradise of hidden roads and a canopy of trees along the road, definitely a perfect escape route. The vistas and roads merged into one panoramic view, graceful trees on hill sides, churches peeked out of nowhere, as the bikers all leaned their metal 'steeds' through the bends. In the shimmering landscape lay a lake with the sun glistening of it catching everyone's eyes. Freedom, that's what it was, freedom from the work, sleep, repeat life that had no excitement. The smell of flora assaulted their nostrils, leaving them with a calm relaxed feeling, calmer than any of them could ever remember feeling before, the sun half behind a cloud, illuminating the sky with a darkened yellow hue. Sheep and cows grazed in the fields creating an idyllic appearance of what the countryside should look like.

As they stormed through quiet little villages, shaking the foundations of stone buildings, rattling windows, scaring the local cats and dogs, people looked up from their newspapers as they sat at small tables drinking herbal tea, the disgust was written over their faces and they sneered at the loud, vibrating streaming mass of brutality, as it roared through the normally twee village, never had the group looked so out of place, weaving through a ribbon of heaven, Jack at the front, prominent and as solid as steel, followed by the 1 % ers who reflected the same menacing look about them, the little pack of Dan's all showed their individuality as they drifted between the cottages chasing the rolling pack of trouble.

As they trundled through the waving countryside roads, Blockhead was looking more and more like Jack, emulating him with shoulders back, chin up and a grimace on his face that could start a fight anywhere at any time. Dan's expression was more pained and worried, with the weight of his life resting on his shoulders, slouched on his bike pensive and stern. Joanne's rosy cheeks and faith that they would be fine, gave her a contented smile, clinging to Dan for the feeling of happiness that she had missed out on throughout her life.

The old Rockers chugging along on the good old parallel twin, battered and scratched from the real reason they rode together today, Benjie stone faced with the experience of life pushing him on, but a feeling inside of dread and sorrow, thinking this it was all going to end in tears! Emily was in despair not wanting to be part of it at all, but her loyalty to everyone meant she kept her opinions to herself as the dust from the tyres gently graze across her weathered and older face, the face of sorrow and fear, for she knew that no good could come of this, not today not tomorrow not ever. Ritchie showed nothing but happiness, he was one stage away from looking like an excited puppy, bouncing head, singing in his helmet and grinning ear to ear, just experiencing the moment not thinking about tomorrow, living second by second and loving it. Indy's chopper put her in a laid back stance, hands high feet out front and her leaning backwards, only wearing a skull cap and a bandana on her head, with flowery silk cuffs sticking out of her leather jacket which were flapping in the wind mirroring the neck scarf waving behind her, she was now cynical and unhappy, not even sure of herself.

"What am I doing here? This is not my world, not my style or even my way, how did I get mixed up in all this? From carefree to running for someone else's life?"

As she sat aboard her chopper, with her flowery nature slowly dying and her soft playful thoughts crumbling in her mind, life was supposed to be fun, supposed to be free and just living. The serious feeling resting inside her was new, never had she felt worry or fears, never ha she felt that she was having to work hard at anything, but work hard they must, mixed up in a life changing moment that could see all them lose their freedom.

As Jack led the pack from the cover under the green canopy of the Cotswolds, the road changed and the air smelled less pure, less rural, more town like. Jack felt more and more uncomfortable as a helicopter flew overhead. Thinking, *"Is this that the mother fucking police?"* he pulled back his throttle, engulfing his senses with petrol head happiness, the sound, feel and smell from his bike created a safe feeling within him, like a mother swaddling her child, his mind smothered with a sense of protection that gave him more confidence than a cocaine fuelled cage fighter.

An arrogance filled Jack as he passed over the motorway looking down on all the caged animals driving nowhere, the bridge was lined with people, banners and cheers so loud that he could hear them over his clattering thumping bike. He turned his head slightly to see one of the banners; it reads *'Knights of the Road'*, crowds were waving and dancing like a Mardi Gras, some people trying to run alongside them, holding their hands out for high fives from the riders, the cheers rising and somebody played a trumpet, with a marching drummer behind him, dressed in a red jacket with brass buckles, the feeling of a party swept across the air, covering the stony bikers with wonderment, but not one of them cracked or showed any emotion, all following Jacks lead, Jack's arrogance hardened him, lifting his chin higher, puffing his chest out.

"Fuck em I will get to my destination, no matter what it takes and who I have to destroy I will get there"

He roared off even faster and the group behind him responded ever obediently, weaving through traffic, undertaking and overtaking, running red lights, no marshals or 'out runners', just attitude and hell for leather riding! Skimming past car mirrors, often one either side of the car, drivers were shaking their fists and sounding their horns in anger as they pushed the bikes through the smallest of gaps, just watching the front wheel, if the front wheel fitted in a gap, throttle back and go!

As they all rampaged over the motorway a sea of bikes, cars and lorries tagged on behind, trying to keep on the back of the group, dangerously overtaking and pushing through, forcing the cars on the road to stop and move off the road, creating the perfect smokescreen as the 4x4 that had been tracking them slotted in the middle of the mayhem. She was calm but angry, her hair unkempt, no makeup and no nail polish, sorrow in her eyes and a tear rolling down one cheek. As she slowly brushed it away she turned her nose up in hatred, forced back the tears and replaced her grief with anger, muttering to herself;

"Fire or water, burn or drown, I will watch you die and spit on coffin"

She was repeating and repeating her mantra like a spell.

As the group headed back into a cloak of tree lined roads, again the pursuing madness grew, bike after bike, car after car, it seemed like every type of vehicle was there to follow them into normally quiet country roads, as they raced past the fields the intensity was increasing with the speed. Riders on horses galloped along in the tree lined fields, jumping hedges and gates as they run alongside the bikes for as long as they could, horses snorting and hooves hammering along the grass, kicking up dirt, adding to the dramatic feeling in the air. The group was expanding by the second, as they all tag on the back, small shed built beautiful polished café racers with clip on handle bars and detailed modifications. All the bikes seemed to reflect the builder of the bikes, bobbers with rear wheels fully exposed and chopped pipes thundering away, personalised with candy and metal flake paints, gold detailing embossed on to engine casing and extensively polished, the 59 wannabe's dressed in old rockers jackets with hand painted detailing, studs and chains, with white socks over boots and white silk scarves floating behind, all dreaming of the 50's ton up boy days, one was even pretending to be the Reverend of the 59 club, flat trackers on knobbly tyres, crotch rocket sports bikes with huge megaphone exhausts, quad bikes mixing it up and terrorising the road, 'mods' on scooters, mirrors and fake fox tails hanging off them, cyclists trying to keep up, some hanging on to the grab rails of bikes being dragged along, runners and skaters the road united them all, on the road they are all one.

Dan gripped his bike tight; Joanne leant forward on to his back, gripping him tighter, not sure if to smile or cry, thinking was this going to be a blaze of glory? Dan's thoughts far darker, much more crushing to his own soul, deeply depressing him as he knew that as he wanted to escape the world and it's 'rat race' in this moment the rat race was chasing him! The very thing he prided himself on not being part of him literally chasing him, trying to escape the herds and sheeple of society, now they chase him to be like him.

Dan's face once again contorted in the pain of the attention, the thoughts of despair crept into his mind.

"All I want is too escape the pandemonium of this fucked up, lost world we live in"

His head was flooded with mixed up pain and confusion, his stomach knotted up and sweat started to run down from his helmet on to his temple, his lips tightened together and a lump formed in his throat. The anguish of the 'shit storm' he had created for everyone, gripping around his neck, his eyes narrowed as his mind formed a plan. He couldn't let Jack fail his people for him or these new friends who were blindly following, as they'd developed a loyalty to him. More and more crowds were gathered along the road cheering and clapping, even holding banners up with Dan's name on, the mayhem caused a reaction in Dan, a reaction of fight or flight, neither one coming out on top with a melee of fight and flight in equal measure leading him to the conclusion he needed to do whatever it took to survive, but do it alone!

Dan ripped the throttle back, the black and chrome beast, even with two riders on, left a black line on the tarmac as he rampaged to the front, rider after rider being passed with the huge raucous engine playing its music to the people, as it charged to the front he pulled alongside Jack and shouted;

"This is my shit. Don't get mixed up in it!"

With that he slotted in front of Jack, unsure what response he would get but still he eased off the throttle, slowing the group down, creating a rhythm all of his own. Out in front of the group he could no longer see any of the people riding behind him. He tried to block out the waves of people standing on bridges with banners looking down at the big beautiful bike, he created himself a sense of calm, taking away the pain like alcohol used to do for him at his darkest moments. He pondered, the love of a man for his bike cannot be compromised, it never does him wrong, never causes him pain, just carries him away in to his hedonistic silent space of sanctuary.

As he rode his love affair deeper in to the tree lined wonderment, he was unaware of just how many vehicles rolled behind him, cabriolets, saloons, pick up's, white vans, flat bed's, 18 wheeler lorries, all joined the cause, nothing else to aim their primordial need for adrenaline and three figure heartbeats at, joining in from their dull, bland, repetitive lives, wanting a slice of the excitement. Dull people in suits, grey and stale, cheered in their cars and giving the evil death stare, they looked out of place in their dull, company cars, unexcited and unchallenged by the daily grind of the rat race, listening to gangster music but wearing nice ties that matched their shirt and suit combinations. The wannabes joined the cause in search of the three figure heartbeats that their work, eat, sleep, repeat routines could never give, in lives that couldn't even come close to waking them up truly. Merely Zombies in their routines, they had lived less in their adult lives than Dan lived in a single week. Joanne over the last few weeks had lived more than any of these 'chasers' but right here right now they felt, they felt more than they normally did, chasing the cause and chasing the dream of excitement that their lives didn't provide.

The trees all lined up, beckoning him on and waving him past, rolling tree lines along the hills opened up to a spectacular clearing, like a rebirth, overlooking the drop down to a flowing river along the road, as his pace slowed, he had totally forgotten about the ever growing procession behind him, as they looped down the road around a hairpin descent, Joanne's mouth dropped as she caught a glimpse of the following group, the line long and varied, more bikes than she had ever seen in one place before. As she tapped Dan on the shoulder and pointed up at the following entourage, even Dan was shocked by the never ending group behind, she leaned forward so Dan could hear her;

"They are all following you; they are all here for you!"

The words trickled down Dan's spine, leaving him cold, only a man who had lived without moral support could see the wonderment that was following him and yet wish he was alone. Not being used to people helping him or being there for him, he couldn't even begin to see why anybody would be following him, holding him up on a pedestal, to himself he was just a mixed up angry Neanderthal who couldn't keep his temper around self-centred and selfish people.

"I am not the leader I am just ahead of the rest running for my life creating a life just like everyone else"

As the confusion and twisted up mental state set into his mind, it toyed with Dan and what he should say, he was desperately trying not to destroy the only person he cared about as she sat behind him, with her arms wrapped around his waist and her head resting on his back, loving him more than he had been loved in his entire life, a man worshipped by many but hated by himself.

As she lay against his broad back feeling protected and safe, her thoughts wandered;

"I am having too good a time to think about tomorrow, tomorrow is another day and I am alive now, what if tomorrow never comes? What if I lay my head to sleep and this is the day I die? Would I be happy with my life? Would I be proud? Right now, in the moment the answer is yes, looking back at my life the answer would be no!"

As the journey edged forward, sweeping from bend to bend, visceral vistas flowed into the feelings of a couple uncertain of where tomorrow would come from, or what it would bring, but the moment was perfect, chasing the sun as it dropped, chasing the dream, a pot of gold with a fantasy and escape from the awful 'rat race' they were caught up in, drifting their minds away from the problems of the day and living in that moment, alive and loving it.

The bikes, vehicles and all modes of transport flowing along the road, they were extensions of them all, a manifestation of personality, they were a happiness, a love, an escape, pleasure and freedom all rolled into one. Dan's just happened to be a big black motorbike, that took him for solitude and coffee where he could clear his head and then sip his hot black coffee while he gathered his thoughts, ready for the pleasure of the ride. Sometimes it took half a tank, sometimes more, but it always cleared his head! Dan would literally give anything to be free and just riding his bike escaping reality, currently a reality that he despised, what he really desired was internal combustion and wind in the face, nothing more nothing less.

The line of vehicles flowed almost silently behind, a graceful representation of the desire Dan had, the desire they all had, they were all following because they all desired the same, carefree enjoyment, a moment of clarity from the busy confusion of life. Leaving behind the worry and the anxiety, just living in that one glorious moment of happiness, soaring high in the sky as free as the birds above them. In that magnificent moment the miles started to roll by, gone are the large noisy crowds and banners, left behind just a sinuous trail of bikes tracking their way behind their anti-hero.

As the twisting line of bikes drifted through the beautiful countryside the cares of all had pretty much vanished, all in a moment, a single moment of their own shared by many. No one noticed the man stood on the hillside watching, a man in a tracksuit with a flat peaked baseball cap staring down at the majestic sight, his eyes red and bulging, his fists clenched so tight his dirty fingernails dug in to his hands. A feeling of wanting to do something, but not sure what he wanted, as he stood alone he watched, doing nothing but staring.

The lone man stood full of misunderstanding, needing to do something but nothing came; he wanted to talk to Dan, to shout, to find out why, to get closure. He couldn't actually summon the strength to do anything but stare, words surged around his head so fast they didn't even make a rational sentence, just noises mixed in with whys what ifs and buts. Rooted to the spot, his teeth pushed so hard together the pain built in his jaw, it's nothing in comparison to his heart, the pain is hollow, sharp yet heavy.

Why did these people love this murderer, the man who took his boy from him? As these words formed in his cerebral melee, the emotions and pain screwed his face up tight, tearing his life away from him, unable to comprehend how he would go on without his boy. As the man stared, the police watched him from afar, watching the man motionless and silent he was different, clearly not a supporter of the cause, just standing with clenched fists. The police were gathered along the way relaying messages to a central co-ordinator, who's only goal was to stop this visual display of solidarity for a murder and arrest the antihero they held so dearly to their hearts. Not wanting to create media frenzy so it can be contained, was almost impossible, but stop this rolling ruckus they must.

Towards the back of the rolling riot of somebodies and nobodies all halfway to nowhere, the 4x4 that had been trailing them since the overnight, picked its way through the nobodies, her ability to not care about anybody determining her driving style, constantly mounting the kerb, nudging other cars out the way as she overtook everything and anything, slowly but surely. Her face now emotionless, stuck with one expression, pale skin and heavily wrinkled, aged by a poor lifestyle, poor or not her life now has one focus, revenge! Trying to shake her pain from her inner most feelings, so she could inflict it all on to Dan, show him how much she hurt and how much Billy hurt physically and mentally on a daily basis, stuck in a cycle of love and hopelessness.

She had dreams of running a second hand shop with Billy, renovating old stuff and selling it for a quick profit small or large, Billy could barely leave the house, his anxiety from the attack consuming him and destroying him, wetting the bed and barely sleeping, his mind as damaged as his body, no longer able to use one of his arms, so badly damaged by Dan's motorbike of pain, the studded tyre removed so much muscle, his arm couldn't even support its own weight and the other arm shaking constantly. Sitting in his chair just rocking back and forth, he just keeps drinking till he can't feel the pain anymore. He avoided his reflection, his skin burned so deeply that one ear and part of his nose had been completely lost. His hair never grew back and neither did his confidence, mutilated beyond recognition, the only friend he had was his daft old Labrador, who never left his side, spending most of the time lying across the Billy's feet.

Her dreams now were broken desires, shattered and unthinkable and her only desire now was to hurt Dan and all of the idiots who followed him, no plan of how, just opportunities to vent her anguish, give her a sense of purposeful power to control the agony that now controlled her. She moved on with no care for anyone, the people she drove passed looked at her confused as to why she pushed her way through, why she did not give any room. *'Move or be moved'* was her style.

The police have started to notice her, she was different, she had a different style about her and she was not here for happiness, which was clear to them all. The female officer radioed ahead giving the registration of the 4x4, instructing them to look out for it and keep track of the battered vehicle. As the police discussed the plan of action, it was clear they were ill prepared and had no plan of action. The female officer sat with a map and a marker pen, plotting the route they had taken and looked at the options of where they may be heading, they would literally be running out of road soon, the sea beckoned.

Leading on this kind of job is new to Tania, but the pressure of the job was not so new, Ms Tania Blackstone had worked hard to be promoted above her male colleagues, many had suggested she had slept her way to the top, but they couldn't be more wrong she had lied cheated and stamped on anyone who stood in her way, her reputation fierce and even the senior bosses were afraid off her, a nasty streak fueled her and her desire to crush any man that tried to show her up or even dare to think they were better than her.

No one at the front was aware of any of the people behind, just 'point and shoot' style riding as the sun slowly dropped, leaving coldness in the air and a silhouette of noise barking into the darkness. Mixed up, tangled up in life is where this all began for Dan, the misconception of youth, fighting with the feeling that his dad did not want him, blaming himself for causing his dad to kill him mum before killing himself, crying himself to sleep for many years, unloved, unsettled and misunderstood. The lack of love he experienced shaped him, made him and ultimately destroyed him, creating addictions to anything that brought him love, anything that made him feel needed and gave himself worth, he was loved by Morris and Dotty, but they could not break down the wall around his heart, cemented by the torture of watching his parents die on the floor in front him, helpless and unable to fix it or stop the pain.

As a young man he had briefly joined the military and felt a sense of belonging, a family of his own, but could not hold a gun without reliving the horror of his dad pointing one at his mum. He would bare knuckle fight anyone, but offer him a gun and he became meek and mild and was eventually discharged from the army on mental health grounds, compounding his feeling of not belonging. He started to find his calm with engines and engineering, if he could fix it or make it better the feeling of belonging and purpose grew stronger. His life spiralled out of control, but with a job in engineering he felt calmed, however only feeling true sanctuary on the road, pushing the limits of life then reflecting on it over a black coffee, adoring his life on the edge with a three-figure heartbeat, the only time he felt, really felt and knew he was living. Without his adrenaline fuelled danger, calmness was impossible. Without his fix of exhilaration and his revelations of life, he felt nothing, just the slow creep of time, waiting for the endorphin filled cocktail of life he desired.

CHAPTER 8:

WHAT IS LIFE?

As the miles rolled by Dan's mind wandered like the road, through a myriad of scenery and sights, pleasant green rolling hill landscapes with satisfying smelling fields of yellow adorning his path, delighting his nostrils and tickling his spirit, coupled with some vile, rank, awful smelling industrial monstrosities, repressive and putrid, the smell of waste attacking his entire body assaulting his nostrils, invoking a sickness and a heavy head, all of his joints literally aching from the mental torture he had endured. Cynical about life, himself and everything he had ever ruined, his empire of shit was really weighing down on him creating a sickness, smelling worse than a silage pit and causing the same reaction in his head as falling into one.

With the awful taste of filth still flaring his nostrils and pulling his face to a grimace, he rolled on carrying the thoughts that tortured him. '*Where next? What next? Who am I? Who do I want to be? Where do I want to be?*' The revelations of his questions spiralled round his head adding to the confusion, mixing his feelings unrecognisably, the only thing keeping him sane, was the spiritual experience that being on his motorbike brought him.

The revelations of his questions make him talk to himself like a counsellor, advising himself as if he was helping someone else with their revelations about their life, counselling himself and adjusting his mental state with just his calm revelatory voice.

As he talked to himself the questions came thick and fast, the answers came even faster, talking to himself honestly with no one else to listen, gave him the realest answers he could get.

As a young man he even called himself the 'Revelator' after his bible-reading father had pushed the book of revelations on to him, making him develop into a logical and chronological person, creating order and sense of his messages to himself, analysing the future events that could happen, war, famine and pestilence, causing affliction and contrasting tribulations, darkening his sun and moon, the wrath had already happened and this was the end as the trumpets sounded, Armageddon was nigh.

The strict bible upbringing he had before his dad destroyed their family, repulsed him and turned him away from the teachings of the bible, favouring the teachings of Odin and believing in Valhalla, even one of his tattoos was Odin with a cross and ravens. Revelating his life was how he survived alone. Even though he often didn't like his answers his tormenting mind gave him, they were real.

Dan's revelatory mind questioned his mortal existence;

What is the Utopian dream? What is the perfect life? What would change the course of man? Is it the social media validations? All the likes and re shares, is that living? Waiting for someone to tell you what you did was right for you? Is that good? Is that true to yourself? Is that the new love? The internet is both constructive and destructive to society, corrupted by the evil people that are power and money hungry, rather than being a resource to learn and make life easier. Is it money or your job title? People ask you what you do for a living so they know how much respect to give you! Should we not all be equal!? We all still take a dump and wipe our ass, in truth we are all the same yet different, we are all the same level at least!

Money is an abstract happiness, a false idol, a false temporary happiness, not a true deep meaningful long lasting contentment, time is priceless but free, you can always get more money but you can't get or buy more time! A rich heart may be shrouded by a poor coat and a poor heart may be covered by an expensive coat, are you spending your time well or are you just letting it disappear?

Dan spoke to himself, knowing he was from an old world where life was different and he liked that, he would not want to be part of the self-obsessed youth of today, or the contended 9 to 5 brigade just existing, he mused deeper into his darkness, because you travelled through your time in life, does not mean you lived. Some people live more in one day than others do in an entire life, big houses expensive meals, 'flash' cars do not make you alive! Many people live till their mid-20's, dying before they are 30 but not buried till they are in their 70's or 80's, many lives are lived yet unlived and many live a robotic, repetitive, dull life. most don't realise this till it is too late to live, time has literally slipped through the hands of life, missed opportunities to live, we all need mundane balance to allow the life to take place, money is a necessary evil, but the undoing of life as we all chase money as if it was happiness, forgetting we don't need as much as we thought we did, just enough to appreciate the smaller things in life, not to try and impress the cheap-suited types who are dressed to impress, these people with less money than they look like they do, as they wear all their money on their backs, around their wrists and fingers literally dripping in all they have, leaving a gaping hole in the happiness of their soul, never experiencing the true meaning of life, freedom and content!

Was Dan slowly becoming the man he should have been? Pleased by his core morals but angered with how he dealt with society the answer was yes but overshadowed by the no, as he ran from his life, trailed by the very society he wanted to escape. The type who valued money and possessions over being alive, chasing the next promotion, chasing the next house, chasing the next car, working so hard the sands of time drift by, escaping the very life they are creating then needing to avoid the reality by blocking it out, as the reality of their time is they need to block out the life they are leading, or take a break from it, as it makes them so tired of life, if it was a good life you wouldn't need chemicals to create a hazy escape from it!

Drink and drugs, why? So they can live in the moment, no past no future just the now. Was there another way? Freedom from the fight and the consumer led anti-life that the modern world brings to us all, corrupting our dreams and polluting our ambition with misguided choice.

The choice to live or exist, the choice to stay or to run always weighed heavy on Dan's mind. Dan's choices were strategically being limited by the ever closing assault from law, order and control closing in the net on the rolling mayhem Dan had started, little did he know that the next few bends would lead him in to an ambush, a tri-party attack from all sides, the 4x4 ever gaining from the rear the track suited man loitering on the hillside and now from a police ambush trying to rip the wheels from the wagon of the vengeful angel, who draws in the nobodies worshipping him and blindly following.

The vengeful black parade was rumbling along aimlessly following, sweeping into a long beautiful bend, ecstasy about to meet the misfortunes which are set out on a junction, a lorry parked up with police in the seat, the huge V8 monster engine running chugging out black smoke from the two large exhaust stacks at the back of the cab, vibrating away ready to pounce with a team of cars ready to block junctions and a solo female officer in charge, she is a passenger in a helicopter above shouting orders into the radios of the team.

As Dan passes the lorry it roars into life, big V8 noise with black smoke pouring from the twin upright exhaust stacks, it vibrates and lurches forward driving straight out into the junction, skimming passed the original group, then cutting off the rest of the 'wannabes' bringing them all screeching to a stop, bikes with tyres screeching, rear ends sliding to the side, crashing into each other, the noise of metal on metal as the exhausts of the bikes clang together, between two over the top polished big money dealership accessory laden cruisers, both with smart full dealer branded gear had collided, the kind of guys who work in the city and wants to pretend they are 'keeping it real' with huge speakers and low mileage, they look at each other now more worried about the damage on the bikes rather than what is happening to the lead pack.

The 'wannabes' see the police presence and go into 'melt down' like the norms that they are, they scatter in all directions terrified that this will upset the balance of their works eat, sleep, repeat lives, fearing repercussions on their precious careers, the pandemonium of the crowd trying to escape is loud and frantic as the police block them in like sheep in a pen.

Police cars and police motorbikes trying to contain the mess and drawing them into one group, the panic of the crowd causing a mass 'bolt' the most adrenaline this group of mixed up car salesman, dentists and accountant types have ever had in their comfortable rich lifestyles, completely engulfed by 'fight or flight' emotions, fear and excitement rolled into one, but missing the most important feeling of solidarity and respect for each other, a group together and separate all at once a meaningless group of nobody cares, with no thoughts left for the cause they originally thought they were part of, leaving Dan and his group to run for the sun.

The track suited man scrambled up a tree to get a better look ripping his trousers as he climbs through the branches, the sharp twigs scraped at his skin as he climbed, he had only one thought to see if the murderer of his son had been laid down by the truck, he didn't want Dan dead but wanted to know he was suffering and imprisoned, for the first time since Dan killed his son at the roadside, he had clarity and knew what he wanted. He wanted to see Dan trapped, a caged bird of prey unable to fly, his wings clipped, Dan living out his years as miserable as he felt to no longer have a son, happiness taken away by Dan, he was now being tormented by the death of his son with every waking second, coupled with sleepless nights and visions of his son being murdered, spliced with images of him playing football as a child, teaching him to ride his first pushbike, the emotion tears a strip from his heart causing him to puke from the tree, nearly falling from his perch, the vomit splashed down the tree and began to pool on the ground, his stomach empty and a vile taste in his mouth, which does not really register as the empty void and foul taste left in his mouth from grief is too strong to be overpowered.

The unspeakable grief of losing a child, outweighed everything the real world could give him, hollow and pained, his life actually ended the moment he saw his son laid out on a mortuary slab, the clinical smell still making him heave every time he remembered the moment, every day since that awful day he has wished to end his life, his unkempt look obvious as no care for himself has been taken since that day, but no strength left to end it, forever twisting and turning in a putrid pool of pain.

As the 'wannabes' wildly tried to escape, the 4x4 with its bull bar pushed passed cars, bikes and anything in its way, escape was not on her mind, catching up with Dan was the only desire she had, her thoughts clouded by the revenge she would like, her dark thoughts fantasising about tying Dan to the tow bar of her car and dragging him along this road, thinking that this would be a start to ease her pain, she kept the 4x4 steered hard to the left, mounting the grass verge and smashing through a wooden fence, splintering the wood everywhere and tearing through the barbed wire that was nailed across the top of the fence, as she 'floored' the throttle the engine lurched into life, drowning out the noise of the barbed wire scratching at the paint as it's flung over the roof of the truck, flinging the vehicle to the right and keeping her foot pressed so hard on the throttle her leg muscle literally felt like it would burst, the tyres struggled for grip, the deep wet mud covering the vehicle in a deluge of brown, the back of the truck sliding violently to the left, wrestling with the wheel she kept her foot hard on the throttle snaking the vehicle across the field, flat out, she was tossed up and down side to side in her seat bouncing over the rough terrain, no thought or care of damage, ripping the green grass from the ground and turning it to a muddy track with a cascade of mud being flung in all directions.

The gate is open to the field but she has not even seen it, at full speed her frenzied driving style smashed her straight though a hedge flattening the hedgerow bouncing out on to the road, her foot still hard down as she races along the now clear road, with the female officer looking through binoculars, thinking;

"Either she wants to rescue the man or kill him!"

Dan is a disillusioned soul in a fucked-up world running from his life, Dan had always tried to escape his early years and was now trying to escape his recent mess of life too, the pit of his stomach gurgling and pained with stress and fear, the fear that this could be the end. That thought soon faded into insignificance when the worry for Joanne and the sorrow of all the others he had drawn into his empire of hurt flooded into him, for him to be causing problems for the people he respected was always a really painful experience, the pain this time was worse, worse as he was hurting the one person who he wanted to save, the one person he loved, the one person he wanted to run away with and start again, treating her like an angel, loving her and caring for her till the world stops spinning.

He had a million dreams held in his mind for their joint road through life, the happiness and hope a polar opposite to the atrocity of his reality with Joanne now, the swirling feeling in his stomach moving up into his throat, burning as the remains of his last meal erupted into his throat and crept into his mouth flooding it with a vile sensation that riots around his taste buds, he swallowed the putrid half eaten meal, burning more on the way down than on the way up, the rage in his mind overpowering the worry and bullshit he was in right now, the search of the future was slipping away from him there was a battle to be won, an escape to freedom, a new life a new way!

Escape or die no in between, freedom or honourable death, the thoughts from his teenage years powered him forward, a slogan on a tee shirt he wore as a boy, it's better to burn out than fade away.

He was ready for what may come, pain or ecstasy, Dan had always had a blurred line between the two, finding happiness in sorrow, good in bad, pleasure in pain and more importantly hope from despair. Ever moving forward, never standing still, reaching for the next thing never satisfied with what was served, you only get what you took and what you created, sit back and wait and you only get the scraps of life, stand up and create and you could have whatever you wanted, setbacks were just problems without solutions, walls that needed ladders. The wild storm of thoughts created a painful mess in his head, his thoughts turned dark, his mood black and his ability to move forward strong again;

"Stand up Dan and be counted, burn out or fade away, live for now and create the future, fuck 'em, stand back world I am coming through!"

Forced to reroute due to the police barricades they pulled in and regrouped, Jack stormed to the front on foot with a menacing stride and a screwed up angry expression on his face, angrily booming out his deep voice;

"For fucks sake! What is this shit storm? We are going to have to split as these bikes are loaded with drugs and we are hot property with all these fucking police attacking us, we need fuel and to fucking run, you guys will be on your own on this one I have to get these drug mule bikes to safety!"

Dan's confused face grimaced with the now normal pained state of being stuck in between a rock and a hard place, wishing he was alone rather than destroying other people's lives, with a large lump in his throat and red bulging teary eyes he looked Jack square in the face;

"Jack you must do what you must do, you have helped me so much and I hope we cross paths again, but go don't let my cradle of shit weigh you down, they chase me not you, disappear into the abyss of this mess, they don't even know you guys exist!"

Jack unusually unable to hold back his emotions his top lip in a quiver his nose twisted up as he fought against showing his emotions, with a large swallow he was a man who refused to cry, he stepped towards Dan holding out one hand for the Viking handshake of bikers and placing the other hand on the back of Dan's neck, he pulled Dan in close bringing their helmets together with a dull thud forehead to forehead man to man, Jack whispered;

"I love you and you are a true brother willing to fight the fight and fight the cause with more morals than I have seen in a man for many years"

Jack swallowed his emotions hard, the gulping noise he made heard by Dan sounding akin to a sinking ship consumed by the ocean;

"Dan you mother fucker, get you and your little pack on that boat as me and lose yourself from this storm, I will regroup and return when this has settled, in this world or in Valhalla under the reign of Odin I will stand by you again as your equal"

And with that, the strong, defiant, Jack was back, standing up straight looking back to his men 'barking' orders;

"Right you mother fuckers, Dan and his pack ride alone, we will regroup and party till this blows over, bring on the food beer and dirty women!"

As Jack tore away on his bike he raised one fist high in the air showing his solidarity for Dan, the loyal 1% ers raced after him kicking up a dust that settled around the remaining group, all mentally flattened. As the dust from the departure settled the fuel tanks were nearly empty like the new life Dan thought he had built.

As Dan started his engine his sorrow pulled his head low, he glanced back at the silent little group, with no words Dan and Joanne gently rode away, leaving the group motionless and dumbstruck, as the beautiful and dirty behemoth of a bike coasted along the road into the next fuel station, Dan trying to nurse the last few drops of fuel from the bike. Ridding the bike now felt empty like his tank, Jack had literally abandoned him, the feeling always hurt him no matter how slight as it brought with it the feelings of abandonment that everyone he had ever trusted had given him.

Standing there pumping golden nectar into his bike, no words were exchanged; the looks between Dan and Joanne spoke volumes. As he walked off to pay for his golden nectar three guys jumped out from the back of a van and wrestled him to the ground, dragging him to the road as a black limousine screeched to a stop. Joanne started screaming and running over to help but was met with a gun to her face and a simple phrase; "*Quiet or die*" the man stood in his expensive suit ripped and dirty from dragging Dan to the ground, as Dan was bundled in to the back of the car still in his helmet, struggling, kicking and fighting, he was also met in the same way but by a man dripping in arrogance, who leaned forward, ramming the barrel of the gun so hard against Dan's nose it cracked and splintered the bone.

With the blood running down his stinging face and his arms twisted so far behind him he can feel his shoulders literally being torn from his body, the burn in the muscles completely immobilising him, he was slumped in the back of the most expensive car he had ever been in, but in far too much pain to enjoy it.

As the suited man lowered the gun he pulled out a silk handkerchief from his top breast pocket, wiping the blood off his gun, he started to talk with a London 'twang' to his voice but interjected with a pretentious posh pretence;

"Look what you have done, this handkerchief is hand stitched and very expensive, you have ruined it with your blood, you need to pay for that, do you know how much money you owe me from the last few weeks?"

The pain in Dan's face as the blood gently rolled down into his beard clouded his mind;

"What? I don't even know you, how do I owe you anything?"

As the suited man dropped back into his luxurious leather seat and sips from a champagne flute he narrowed his eyes and stared deep into his Dan's eyes;

"Not only did you break into my church, you fucked your whore on my dining table and damaged my priceless candelabras, you broke the hinges on a box made in Tibet in the15th century by a small group of monks, you killed one of my top men, stole my money and you took a priceless Tibetan piece of art a 'Thangka' given to me by a wise old monk as he died in my arms. How do you owe me anything? You are lucky not too be wired up to the mains in that church, you are lucky I have had to chase you across the fucking country"

Dan's face twisted in horror as he remembered the cloth with the art on it that he took with the money.

"That monk was called Tenzin, I pulled him from the jaws of a snow leopard, He gave me that painting and blessed my soul, he asked me to keep it with me and told me it would keep me from danger and I want it back!"

The gunman outside the car stood with a crying Joanne, as she watched the blacked out window slowly go down and Dan's beaten face appear;

"Joanne get the money and the painting from the bag"

Joanne let out an almighty wail, never had she seen her strong man so weak or heard him so scared, his voice croaked and quivered like a terrified boy. As she ran for the duffel bag on the back of the bike, she stumbled and tripped hardly able to keep her balance, with her mental world rocked too, her world now crumbling like the walls of Jericho.

As she clumsily ran back with the bag, fumbling to find the painting, the door of the car was flung open and Dan was bundled out on to the floor, rolling head first along the ground bashing his helmet as he rolled on to his back, the fall had scuffed the paint on the helmet and he was covered in dirt and dust, leaving him with a dull headache and the blood from his nose now covered in a dark sticky dust. the suited man slowly appeared from the car, looking impossibly tall he reaches into his suit jacket and pulls out his gun again, towering over Dan with his shoes reflecting the lights brightly in the high sheen polish, the impeccable suit with the sharp edges waving in the wind;

"I am not fucking around give it to me! Or watch your cheap wench die in your arms!"

CHAPTER 9:

WHAT MAKES YOU ALIVE?

Unable to retaliate, unable to retort, fighting back the tears, the insult to Joanne rubbing salt in his already gaping wounds, Dan lay in the dirt with a headache like no hangover could match. The dull throb beat in his head, drumming out pain on every beat, the blood poured from his swollen, broken nose into his beard, the pain in his face throbbing and the pain in his nose sharp. The tall suited man stood above, looming over him sneering down his perfect long nose, his suit perfectly pressed and pinstriped, making him look even taller, he pointed his gun directly at him;

"Move and I will put you down like the dog that you are! You are way out of your depth here small fry! You stole from me, killed my top man and now you lie here in the dirt, one trigger pull from death, all in my control. Look at you, you're pathetic, a mouse of a man!"

Dan's rage was building as he was unable to deal with the dishonour and the insult, his brow furrowed and his lips pursed trying to control an outburst.

As Dan struggled to control himself, trying to avoid that trigger pull, Joanne rushed over with the bag spilling its contents on to the floor. The familiar sound of a V twin lurched its way in to the fuel station *'pop-pop-pop-pop potato, potato, potato'*, the unmistakable noise almost asthmatic as Indy partially closed the throttle, the engine gleaming in the sunshine, Indy now drove straight at Dan a fixed icy stare pierces right through him, he knew he had disturbed her carefree world and made her harden, as the straight piped 70's chopper bounced across the bumpy surface, the angry hippy was aiming her skinny chopper front wheel at Dan.

In horror he watched the wheel coming towards him, turning his head away unable to believe the betrayal of someone so pure, toughened by the destruction of her flowery world, dropping his head Dan turned away from the impact, his head tilted forward and lower than his pride, Joanne stood rooted to the spot, a look of horror and disbelief ripping her face open, her mouth stretched wide but silent, her eyes the size of dinner plates and full of tears, Indy's face was mean, determined and angry, pulling on her rabbit ear chopper handle bars, leaning the bike as far as she could, dragging a peg in the dirty dusty ground with sparks flying from her peg, she hit the tall suited man, narrowly missing Dan, the long raked out forks flexing and bouncing over the body of the suited man, tearing his suit at the seams as he was bundled to the ground, his gun flung to the side and his arms flailing as he fell to the floor, keeping the throttle pinned, her rear wheel mounted his head, the soft tyre of the hardtail chopper rolling up and deforming over his face and as the V twin's brute power continued to thud away, the rear wheel spinning his head violently sideways, killing him instantly.

As Indy struggled to hold her bike under control she was tossed around on her saddle barely holding on to the bars as the bike bucked and kicked violently, tossing her in the air like an amateur bronco rider on a professional bucking bronco, she was no longer in control just hanging on as the bike starts to 'tuck' under, she screamed;

"Daaaaannnnn ruuuunnnn"

Indy dropped the bike and slid along the floor, her jacket grazing the ground and gripping the surface pulling her to a stop, the thick old cow hide leather jacket doing its job and saving her skin, as the bike slid from between her long slender legs with the rear wheel still spinning, blood had been splattered on to the chrome, from the neck snapping assault. The rest of the group charged in after her in a disorderly deafening whirl of noise, riding around the wrinkled suited body on the floor creating enough dust to screen the dead body from sight, they skidded to a stop, surrounding Indy who still lay on the floor, Blockhead jumped off his bike, grabbed the gun and pointed it at the other henchmen, he looked over his shoulder;

"Dan get the fuck out of here!"

He had never held a gun, he looked like he had done this before, but in his stomach he was wrapped up in knots, scared sick and hoping not to have to pull the trigger at all.

Dan grabbed Joanne by the arm, dragging her to the bike, gripping her far too tightly and sending pain shooting up her arm, he threw his leg over his bike, Joanne likewise slings herself onto the bike, nearly taking them both off the other side, Dan grimaced with aches and pains all over, his vision slightly blurred, his head swaying as he tried to clear his head, he could barely hold all three of them upright, as the bike fired its enormous engine, wailing its roar into the air. Dan was fixed unable to go, the bike roared and Joanne screamed get me out of here! His gaze fixed on Indy with a tear rolling down his cheek mixing with the blood, drawing a salty bloody taste into his mouth. Indy now on her feet gesturing for Dan to leave and shouting;

"Dan ride, ride, goooooooooo"

In a mix of fear, pain and distress he was once again running for his life, this time literally, feeling like the whole word had just collapsed in on him, dragging his mind into a mental stupor, pain now flooding down his cheeks as he rode, no longer able to control his emotion, broken and distraught, piece by piece collapsing and falling apart, each piece tearing a void into his soul as it fell, he was a fallen angel who a few days ago felt like he had it all, who now literally is at the end, no fight left but his morality telling him to get Joanne to safety.

The little group surround Indy all checking her over and asking her if she is okay, she looks over at the twisted and beaten face of the suited man and literally falls to her knees, wailing as the young free mind of a loving hippy dies, never again will her heart beat with purity, never will her eyes close without remembering the evil running through her veins as she killed a man, she was now no freer than anyone shackled to the torture and hatred of the modern world she tried to reject, but it's found her, chased her down and won.

As they got Indy on her bike and they once again chased after Dan for one reason and one reason alone, loyalty! The suited man's dead body now being dragged from the small pool of blood on the floor, with his suit jacket split open and his trousers ripped, the henchmen pulled his body in to the limousine, as the door closed it slowly drove away as if nothing had happened carrying with it, it's dirty hidden secret, moving away with an air of class, in contrast to the henchman's van driving away like it was on fire, in a spinning high revving display of panic.

The black behemoth of a bike was like a bulldozer large and imposing thundering along, it did not judge, it did not question, it did not feel, it just did what it was asked to do,

'Carry me away sweet sister, carry me far away', as it picked up speed the serenity of Dan's mind started to return, the pain of his broken nose throbbing away and the pain of his broken mind sent pain into his temples, mixed in with the cerebral *free-for-all* of his mind, Joanne gripped him tight, eyes closed with her head pressed onto his back.

The police helicopter watched from a distance and the hardened police officers all sat in silence as the noise of the helicopter blades spin round taking over the moment, shocked by what they had seen, unable to comprehend the unreal sights they had just witnessed. As the pack reformed again as one and so it continued, the rolling death march of these bikes seemingly could not be stopped.

Leaving behind a tragic wake of misery as the death march gathered momentum, way behind them the track-suited man, was still standing in the tree unable to go on as he watched from afar on the hillside, having watched Dan escape while the rest of the followers were cut off and trapped. His grief slowly consumed him, bubbling up like a sickness creeping up inside his soul, causing immeasurable pain inside the hollow emptiness of him, the hollowness only a parent who has lost a child could feel, a hole cut out that passes from front to back all the way through, leaving nothing behind, a feeling of something missing. He wanted Dan to be dead, but hated himself for wishing pain on others, a good man that loved to feel happiness and not wish pain and sorrow on anybody.

He was a soft man who did no harm, who brought up a boy with a no rules style, the only rule was no rules, just enjoy, love was priority and fun was to be had rather than rules. The boy had grown up not understanding respect or guidelines; he had made his father happy but had no respect for others. His father could not see the damage he had done by not creating a balance of love and fun coupled with cause and consequence, as he removed his zip up tracksuit top and tied it around the branch above his head, he loved his son and hated Dan. Unable to deal with his opposing feelings, the uncontrollable grief now took hold, as it climbed up his body, pressing on his gut, tightening around his lungs till he could hardly breath, his heart felt nothing but as the grief stricken feeling coupled with the mixed up love and hate reached his mind, it felt like two hands inside his skull pushing down on to his brain, the pain more than a human can stand torturing him, his own mind had turned against him with no heart left to argue against the voice in his head, telling him how awful he was for wanting Dan dead, no better than any murderer for wanting to bring pain to someone.

The voice in his head was dark and strong ranting at him telling him if he has no worth, nothing to give, nothing to live for and no good can come from his life, he is a failure and a hideous person, the opposite to the person he wanted to be so pure and loving. With this deranged dark lord beating him down crushing his mental strength, till he stood there with tears streaming down his face, wailing in mental pain trying to argue back with all his happy memories of life, the dark overlord in his mind was too strong and as the mayhem in front of him slowed to a calmness, the vehicles one by one had fled, leaving a stillness, he wanted to feel a calmness too. As he stepped from the branch, he had one end of his track suit top attached to the branch above and the other around his neck, his mind figuratively broken, his feet fell from his perch, his weight dragging him sharply downwards, the jolt literally snapped his neck and the next few moments of peace are bliss for him as he slowly slipped away, but he left behind a trail of destruction for all that surrounded him, if only his heart could have fought back hard enough to show him the next few days and weeks as the family not only now had to bury one family member but two, maybe he would have not taken that final step.

As he swings back and forth in the tree at peace with himself, he is unaware of the pain he leaves behind, he had a loving wife who idolised him, treating him like her hero, he had a younger brother who worshiped him and looked up to him as a leading light in his life, due to the sickness in his mind, caused by the death of his son, he has destroyed an already grief stricken family who had to endure a second police visit to bring the same speech of grief in a week, but this time it's suicide and seen as selfish rather than a sickness, a man that needed help and could not see passed the darkness to his family, if he could have visualised their grief, maybe he would not have killed himself, maybe his family could have stood together as one and helped him passed his darkness.

The darkness that now sat in his now calm soul swinging in the tree, not his fault but the ripple effects of life had chased him and countless moments from everyone's life had merged into that moment of catastrophe, actions from anyone could have help to avoid the suicide, the carless actions from his son, the anger from Dan, or the parenting from the family. Which ripples led to this, which one would have needed to be changed, who would know? But in reality we are all one wrong decision from a bad ripple effect

Dan's three figure heartbeat was now dangerously high and his back soaked in sweat, fleeing with his life running from danger, in that fight or flight caveman style, running from the sabre-toothed tiger, really feeling his heart beat, that primordial buzz, that adrenaline filled cocktail of life. The thoughts tormenting him again *'If you're not actually running for your life with sweat pouring off you and a heart beating hard enough to bounce of your rib cage, are you even alive?'*

The modern world was so easy and assisted, less and less hard work to endure, with an app and a computer to do things, gone was the daily release of the adrenaline chemicals that floated around our body, creating gratification and satisfaction and as they are used and then dissipate giving a long lasting calmness. We were programmed to seek out danger, to use these chemicals. Life no longer facilitated this regularly, leading to boredom and quick fixes of short lived satisfaction, that never really 'hit the spot' in need of the primitive release, the thrill of the hunt and the achievement. This is what Dan and his little pack were actually searching for, excitement and thrills, danger and exhilaration, spurring an urge to move forward to discover and develop, forever moving forward, like the life of a rolling stone.

The feeling of being on the bike was a feeling of freedom from real life and an excitement that couldn't be explained only experienced, the exhilarating feeling on a bike was difficult to match day to day, as the mundane cycle of life took place, the feeling in a cage on the road is not even comparable, a protected air-conditioned filtered numbness, taking people one step away from the real feelings, more so as cars became designed with comfort in mind not excitement. On the bike it was all real, exaggerated and intensified, seconds from danger, death or delight, the feeling of knowing this was dangerous is exciting and a feeling of unmatched joy, releasing the satisfaction within, so many addictive chemicals, all natural and produced 'in house' by your own mind, real, felt experiences not just viewed from a car window, as leaves whistled passed you they are closer, as they hit you in the chest you could feel them, smells were stronger, light was brighter, you are closer to the tarmac, feeling its roughness rather than the softness, the excitement of speed and danger combining to an all-encompassing smash and grab excitement.

Humans and in particular men were hard-wired from thousands of years ago, needing to run from the sabre-toothed tiger and experience the joy of escaping the near death excitement that now came from leaning closer to the tarmac and taking risks, edging closer to the road, edging the knee down towards the road in a bend and powering forward feeling the rear tyre struggling for grip, skill levels adjusting the throttle and weight all in one to keep the bike shiny side up, whilst exiting the bend, troubles are left behind as they are outrun by joy and excitement maximised as the adrenaline cocktail floods throughout the mind. In that moment, you have achieved, you have got away and ran from the tiger, really feeling ALIVE! It was so far away from the sofa surfers' nightly stagnation in front of the TV.

Even cleaning the bike or adjusting parts on it was exciting, the anticipation of what will come next, where it will go next, what might happen, where could you go and what could you do? The bike is both life and a freedom giver unlike anything else, used for everything from the mundane shopping trip to a holiday. On the bike nothing was mundane, nothing was normal everything was exciting, even going to fetch a pint of milk was exciting on a bike, although sometimes that excitement meant the pint of milk from the local shop turned out to be a shop 50 miles away! Life was never dull when you had a bike, stop for a bag of chips and people will want to talk and ask about the bike, or take it away in to the wilderness and escape the norms questioning; *'How fast is it mate?'* the bike was literally a life giver to whoever decided to climb aboard, changing life forever, an addiction leaving the rider needing more and more.

As the pack trawled on, the news of the vengeful parade is no longer that of an antihero, but that of a murderous thug on the run, terrorising the countryside and assaulting the happiness of all in his wake, the news now running the headline, *'Killer Biker Rampage'*. How quickly the media had turned on him, like Bonnie and Clyde they portrayed a romantic free lifestyle of power then a reminder of the evil they have done. The remaining charge forward for the crossing to escape was now the singular thought in Dan's mind, everything pushed to the back, sole survival and freedom intoxicating him, driving him on.

The followers, 'wannabes' and hangers on all sneered at the very epitome of what they believed was wrong with society, led by the news, the media and the TV telling them that Dan is a criminal, the minds of the weak changed easily. Dan lived by the old rules, like those of the Wild West; if a man needed killing for doing wrong a man needed killing. Dan tortured by his own mind as ever, forced himself to believe he did right, avoiding the doubt as he tried to protect his fair maiden. In his head he was a knight on a stallion, rescuing his fair maiden from the sheriff and retreating to his kingdom, a kingdom he needed to rebuild.

The charge forward was fast and uncontrolled, almost frenzied, the little pack almost unable to keep up as Dan rampaged through villages with his throttle wide open, then shut, wide open then shut, the exhaust barking as he weaved around cars and ran red lights not waiting to see if it was clear, just charging through. As each village watched the exit of the black behemoth of a bike, they tutted and shook their heads, returning to their sanctuary and their worlds, just glad the nuisance has passed.

The female officer in the helicopter now high above, so high the helicopter is unnoticed, she floated gently passed, talking on the radio ordering road blocks and armed police, gathering them together, strategically placing them on the route that Dan must be heading towards, he must be trying to cross the channel the road is going to end and he will have nowhere left to run.

The female officer was now on the radio telling her superior;

"I can't let this man go, he can't get away, the law must be respected and he is the representation of a middle finger up to the law if we let him go everyone might think they can run amok, do as they please, be free. It would be anarchy! I will not let some small-time deranged criminal think he can do as he pleases! I am the going to stop him, dead if need be, in a wooden box is better than on the news free as if he is better than me! The public need to see the news from their safe armchairs, so they stay there and don't try to join him again!"

Sat alone in a wingback arm chair, an old man was smoking his pipe drinking a fresh cup of tea, the teapot stood on the table with a tea cosy keeping it warm, just like his wife used to do. Leaning back, dropping biscuit crumbs over his chest, knowing she would have scolded him and complained about his mess, he would have given anything to hear her voice one more time, she was harsh and to the point, but she loved him and showed it daily and he loved her more than he could explain.

Reminiscing of being in his shed listening to his radio, working with his adopted son and showing him how to build the best of the 50's racing bikes. The best of the old bikes, a mix of the best frame and the best engine the perfect race winning bike. Telling him stories of racing these kinds of bikes when he was a teenager racing from café to café and even down the A1 all the way to the café in London, a 'Ton up Boy' for real, he had raced them all from the top of the A1 and even one faithful Whitsun day to Brighton in 1964, showing mods on little scooters who was boss.

Passing on his stories with his knowledge of engineering were some of his best memories, especially when his wife came out all tight lipped and wobbly tits, arms crossed, complaining and shaking her chest from side to side asking; *"How much longer will you be in this shed?"*. No matter what she said when he looked at her all he saw was a beautiful face, his love and his girl his partner in crime, she never moaned when I kicked that mod of his scooter for calling her a 'slapper' oh no a very different story that one, her hero that day.

As he lay there listening to his radio blaring out sounds of the 60's instantly his mind slipped back to the good old rockabilly days swinging his lady around the dance floor showing her he was her man and she was his girl. As he travelled back to a time when he was the king of dance floor with his queen, so much so his foot was till tapping on the floor even after the music on the radio had faded into the news.

The news ended his happy hazy hedonistic place, the voice on the radio very traditional, unionist voice;

"A deranged Yorkshire biker has stormed his huge black motorbike across the south of the country leaving a wake of death and violence in his wake, the police can't seem to stop him, although the huge pack

of followers has been stopped, with many arrests. The armed forces have been called in to stop him now before he reaches Poole Harbour"

The news struck a cold fear through him, his wrinkled arms with all the hair now stood on end, his mouth wide open as he thought; *'It must be, it can only be......Dan!'*

Dropping his china cup, the floor shattering it and exploding the contents all over the floor, splashing against his leg and his favourite armchair, he thought; *'I should have been there for him, he had nobody no parents no family and no friends, I have let him down badly I owe him'*

With a stride of a man 20 years younger, he stormed out of the door dressed in his combat boots, black combat trousers and a white top, hugging a body that was ripped and lean 40 years ago, but now losing the battle with age. Morris had never let age get in his way; he flung open the shed door and stared at his bike, polished silver tank, black detailed badge, café racer seat, clip on bars, with a red frame and a sidecar outfit attached.

Morris loved preparing his bike to start, *'A little tickle on the carbs'*, two small slow kicks on the kick start and one final kick with a bit of throttle, the high compression 650cc pre-unit engine, unfiltered mono block carbs with bigger jets, engaging with the air fuel mix and as it fired up, it literally breathed fire and ticked over really high on those jets, giving Morris a big satisfied smile, thinking; *'I built that'* as it 'puts' and vibrates like an angry little man in a fight.

"Time to make me proud my old friend, I need you more than ever now, pick me up and carry me away, just like you did in the 60's with Dotty in the chair wearing my silk white ton up boy scarf around her neck. 'Be good be fast, be my good ol' friend, we must fix

this for Dan, just like he fixed you, time after time, well here is our time to repay our debt to him before it's too late'.

CHAPTER 10:

LOVE AND DESPERATION

As Morris rode one of the loves of his life he felt a warmth, he remembered the real true love of his life, his soulmate Dotty, but his happiness was short lived the pain of failure, of not being there for Dan to guide him or support him and not being there to protect his wife in her darkest final hour. As the bike flowed through the cold air some of the pain and regret was blown away, not enough to make him happy about abandoning Dan, but nothing would ever take away the pain of losing his lover, his flower, his special lady, his best friend!

The regret of not being there for Dan weighed heavy on his shoulders, but he was not ever there for himself either, he couldn't face life without his flower, her death had crushed him instantly and in one moment his heart had stopped, his soul had died and his mind had fallen apart. The moment she died was the moment Morris died too, he just had the unbearable curse of remaining without her.

The empty nothingness he had at the time of her death was insufferable and he did what he knew he had to do to survive. Immediately after the funeral he had disappeared to find himself again, a rebirth and a restart. In the first few weeks after her death he travelled across Europe sleeping in his sidecar, crying the whole night, as this was his beautiful wife's seat not his. Many times he had planned to kill himself and many times he nearly did, the thoughts coming and tormenting him and taking him literally seconds from disaster, wrestling with wrong and right, the grief was too much to bear, every moment ticked by like a huge rucksack on his back dragging him down, every moment clouded by the vision of his flower crushed on the kitchen floor. As he tracked his way across Europe, he just kept the sea on his left and decided to ride until he could forget his pain.

Every mile the pain worsened with no destination in mind, he just kept moving on, as the memories of Dotty who had not been dead a month stirred around in his head, the floods of happy memories he tried to remember could not touch him he was far too broken. The relationship between Morris and Dotty had been the quintessential perfection; they did have their relationship ups and downs but it was always true love.

Each time he saw her from the moment he stared at her across the dance floor at the youth club, to the moment he left for baking supplies on her last day was pure love stronger than anything always sending quivers down his spine, tears of happiness welling in his heart as his flower smiled back him, he would do for her and she for him too. They had one dream, one life and one direction, the thought was too much for him to cope with as he ran the bike into the hedge, bouncing over the rough edge of the road and up a grass embankment, throwing mud up in the air, splattering him with cold sharp stones and grit, being whipped at by the branches till he hit the fence and was tossed from his second love, his shed built bike. As he lay there with the bike now silent, his mind weeping and his heart dead, he prayed for the first time in decades, please Lord or Lucifer I don't care which take me now, do as you please with me I have nothing to give and nothing to lose, you took my everything when you took her from me.

As the snow started to fall on him, the cold drops of ice touched him in a way he never expected, Dotty was always happy when it snowed, she loved it, Morris pulled his face from pain to a tight contortion, pulled himself from the dirt and dragged his bike and sidecar out of the bushes.

"Dotty wants me to carry on, this is her message to me, I would do anything for her I would do literally anything she asked"

Morris adored her daily dead or alive, every day after they had met was a dance of love, every step a Tango or a Waltz, the looks and half smirks between them just pure happiness and fun. He surprised her regularly with anything he thought would make her smile, she cherished him back in every way every day, age had only made them stronger, they had endured hardships and fights and repaired them all. Morris was good at fixing everything mechanical, but he learned all he knows about life and love from Dotty. The aching abyss left by her departure was made worse as it was not her time, she was taken too soon, that thought was hard to cope with, every heartbeat feeling like an engine with a carburettor blocked with stale fuel. The only thing Morris knew better than Dotty was engines, she literally took him in many ways from a boy to man.

She had found him, but since her death he was lost again, as he rode thorough the worst weather trying to leave his pain behind, no real thought for Dan as he rode away from his grief searching for solitude, till he could take no more and set up camp at the foot of the Harz Mountains. As he now rode back down this road on his way back to England to help Dan, every mile brought with it a memory that he had been through 20 years ago on this road flooded with tears on the way to his sanctuary, he said he would never leave, but Dan deserved better and Dotty had cared for him like a son, she loved him more than her own life and would never hear a bad word against him, he was in her eyes sent from God, a divine intervention, for her to rescue from his awful parents. So now he must return and save him!

Before Dan came to them, Dotty night after night had wanted to go next door to tell them not to scream and shout like this in front of their son, the walls were thin and every word heard as Dan's dad abused his mother both verbally and physically, for some new reason every night, but there was never a real reason, apart from his sick, disturbed, narcissistic view of his family that he treated like new recruits to his platoon, to break down and destroy for his own feeling of self-worth. Dotty always wanted to go next door and stop him, she was feisty and strong, but loving and beautiful in every sense of the word, her physical beauty dazzled Morris, but her inner beauty made him fall in love and never stop loving her.

The memories of Dotty were always strong, his true love was missing everything about a her good and bad, he even missed those moments when he had been out for hours working on his bikes, to return to the kitchen to be greeted by Dotty with a stern look on her face, he read it and no words were needed he knew he had a comment coming;

"And where do you think you have been? While I have been slaving over the stove....you love those bikes more than me!"

With a smile and one kiss on her neck and a gentle whispering in her ear;

"You are my only love, they are nothing compared to you"

The moment was beautiful as she melted in to his arms; she knew just what to say to create these moments and Morris played into her game every time.

As he rode to save Dan he stared at his left gloved hand, he had never removed his wedding ring not even once, he was proud of his love, for those who work at love, love never died, love never faded, love outlived the lovers and lived on as stories passed on from parent to child, people who are shown love have love, people who are shown evil have evil, Dan had lived though both the hatred from his father and the love of his mother, finished off by Dotty's love, but Dan's evil streak was only buried by the sheer amount of love he was shown, not replaced he had both and both were strong.

The love he had for Dotty though the decades had grown like the oak trees in the park, he dreamed of growing old together reminiscing over stories of the good old days. He would have dived headfirst in to any danger to protect her; he would have died for her rather than lied to her. It had been so long since he held her in his arms, his tears were regular and his mood swings frequent as he imagined her alive, creating ecstasy but as the realisation it was just a fantasy came into focus he crashed down harder than he could handle, a broken heart was not repairable like his old motorbike.

Morris lived most days like Dotty was still alive, often talking to her, telling her what was on his mind and what he fancied for dinner, unable to comprehend she was gone, she was still the only one for him and he still bought her favourite flowers and kissed her photograph each night before he went to sleep, as he drifted away the band played and he danced with his love once more, reunited in his dreams they were lovers on the back row in a cinema or taking picnics in the woods. His love had never lessened for her, even after her death he fell deeper in love every time he saw her in his mind, he was like a teenager besotted by her, the only woman in his dreams, even death did not part them, the vows they took meant everything, but little did he know his love would outlast the truth of the vows.

The rain in his heart was cold and dark, each raindrop bigger and heavier as they chipped away at his strength, but the love that he has was strong as he drifted off to sleep chasing away his new friends the darkness and the shadows. The sorrow returned every morning as he woke to an empty pillow, an emptiness that drowned his mind as the reality without her rained into his head. The true love, the rarest love, it wasn't easy and several times they'd nearly lost it and people doubted they would make it, but they did. He took great sanctuary in the thought; as she died in her last moments of anguish lay on the kitchen floor, her heart was full of love and she died at peace, now she was waiting for her love to come to her when his time came. He was shackled to her, he had the key but wouldn't undo the chains, he wouldn't release himself and in his silence he thought of her, his pride was lifted and his heart filled, but her memories were now like the wind, drifting over his shoulders as he chased her memory, never able to catch them or hold her once more, every reflection he saw taunted him as he aged without her, being without her was torture, all he wanted now was to be at peace with her, to be joined again for all eternity. The time to join her was close but Morris had one last thing that she would want him to do before he stood still in the moment and became at peace, joined in eternal death and happiness, forever dancing in the sky of his love.

As Morris rode harder and harder, fighting with the difficulty of riding a sidecar outfit fast, he had often joked with Dan: that those crotch rocket lovers knew nothing of bravery till they have tried to wrestle with one of these at speed. Accelerating the bike pulled the bike left and braking it pulled it right, you steered more with the throttle and brakes than anything else, it took lots of skill and timing to get this outfit round tight county roads, sometimes having to accelerate when you actually should be braking.

The road was hard, but so were the thoughts in the head of Morris as he rode through multiple countries to get to Dan. His mind 'stirred up' an angry questioning monster, with the hatred aimed at himself

"Why had he left Dan? Why had he been so selfish? Why had he not gone back to check on Dan? Why had he left till it was maybe too late to see Dan? What if he could not make it in time and Dan gets killed?"

As the beautiful noise of his twin engine rumbles on, the noise in his head is horrible, literally attacking him, destroying him and creating a black cloud in his mind.

The monstrous questions now came thick and fast:

"How would Dotty have felt? Would she have left Dan till now? Could she have saved him from himself?"

The torture in his mind growing with every mile, an army of troops had gathered to attack him, a battle was taking place in his head, slowly breaking him down piece by piece creating a mind that had attacked itself, a mind that needed to be freed from itself, a mind that needed an escape, to a far of place of solitude, the road that Morris travelled on was wonderful, but his blackened mind only saw darkness as it clouded over him engulfing his spirt. Morris kept on his road of pain, for the sake of Dan and the memory of Dotty, one focus one life and that life was Dan's.

The road Dan was on was even worse that the one Morris was on, he was riding like he was on the death road to Valhalla, both desperate men on desperate journeys, but Dan's was close to the end of the line. The way Dan rode, he could lay his threesome of bliss brawn and beauty down on the road at any time. A wild man of the road is beyond wild, reckless and frantic, no thoughts no calculated risks, just a frantic frenzy of fear as he tears along the road on the death march, death or glory will be found on this road today, he will be just another tale to tell good or bad. Dan started to chant to himself;

"If I die, I die well, in a blaze of glory or not at all!"

This was not a place for a pillion to be and Joanne knew it. Dan was throwing the bike around; his face clear for onlookers to see in his open face helmet, stern and defiant yet scared. Gone was all the usual precision and skill, replaced with frantic lunacy, throttle wide open or closed, no in-between no checks or waiting at junctions, as he appeared in the road in front of cars. Joanne had her head down and her eyes shut, the cars swerved to miss him, often hitting each other and crashing into lampposts. As he raced forward like a man with a 'death wish' he left devastation behind him once again, broken glass and coolant all over the road as cars now marooned all over the road, steam pouring out of them, the scene looking like a war zone.

As Dan wrestled to get the three of them to safety, he knew the only one he really cares for is Joanne, fearing that they can't make it alive, knowing that actually he had fell in love, but the thought of it terrified him, the thoughts were rampaging through his mind; *'If I am going to do this I should do it alone, with all this risk she should be free, free of me and all the pain I will bring I always bring pain that what I do.'*

Stamping on the rear brake and violently causing a rear wheel skid, tearing the loose tarmac from the road and leaving a black line of rubber, the smell of melting rubber wafted up in to his nostrils and Joanne was flung forward on to his back, caught unaware that he would stop so violently;

"Joanne this is it. I can't risk this ride might take you to your death, this could be freedom but more likely our death, we are at the end of the line, there is no more. I love you too much to risk your life"

Joanne's eyes filled with tears and her heart unfolded like the wings of a butterfly, she had been so desperate to hear Dan say the three little words of love, her body melting and her mind drifting away to a paradise far away from where they are now. As quick as Dan melted her heart and desires, he had smashed it down again crushing her mentally, creating more pain than she had ever felt before;

"Joanne you have to get off let me do this, if it works I will send for you, if I die at least I won't have hurt you"

Joanne could barely get her words out as tears streamed down her face.

"Joanne, I have to save you not destroy you, this could be the eternal run for the sun or possible death I love you too much to lead you into this mess"

Joanne's face screamed enragement before she even opened her mouth, she should be ecstatic from the love Dan had for her instead she was furious at the thought of separating from him so soon into this love affair, one she thought Dan would never become part of;

"And I love you too much to let you go into this mess alone! I would rather poke out my eyes than watch you ride away. Together forever, till death us do part, forever riding the road of life alive or

dead together we will be! I am here for the long ride, so take me with you and make it good. If this is our last ride it needs to be hell or high water. I want the ride of my life!"

Dan sat silently subdued, the thoughts wildly ravishing his mind, unable to make sense of anything, the bike ticking away as much as time itself, moving on without him.

"Time to be the star in my own life! Fuck this shit, we ride for death or glory now!"

Dan's contorted mind mixed with all his emotions, not able to think straight, not able to focus, not able to keep his three-figure heart beat down. His usual response was to run, as nobody mattered to him, but now Joanne mattered. For the first time in his life love was clouding his judgement, wishing he could save her but this could be the final ride the final moments of his life, ended before he has found happiness and sanctuary with Joanne. Trapped in a corner like a rat, fight and flight, attack or be attacked, the surreal and clouded judgment in his head was causing a dull moment in his mind, a moment of mixed decisions and with that mix of judgment he rips back his throttle once again.

This time he was different, this time more in control, this time he was wild, but purposeful. Having had no real desire for a mother or a father as he grew up, hating his dad for killing her and himself, growing up without a maternal bond had hardened him to life and love, deep down he had wanted the love but never really understood it, never really allowed his vulnerability to show ever again, but buried it deep down, even Dan had needed his mother and right now would he be in this place if he had her? Would he be different? Would he be running for his life? Who knows but right now Dan could do with something to rein him in, something to control his wild mind.

Rebellious delight was written across his face, this was his moment, he had no fear of death and no fear of life, and he had no fear of anything or anybody. With life flashing before him and the bell tolling for his life, he was outwardly hard but internally weakened, his subconscious begging for his mother to take away the pain, take away this rebellious delight he had, melt him, calm him and control him. The thoughts started to infiltrate his cold hard mind, *'Mamma I need you, mamma I am lost, mamma I have done wrong, I may be on the way to you soon and I may need you, I am a lost boy from a lost family. So take me from this sickened life I have, take me away to my sanctuary'.*

Dan's riding had become careless again, fraught and frantic, making mistakes and near misses as he ran from himself and everything he carried in his mind, a mind that has done him proud but also destroyed him. Understanding his own mind was both a gift and a curse, dragging him down and wanting more, rather than idle contentment for what he had got. Each turn he made, was almost the last, each turn he made nearly killed them both, each turn a brush with death, pedestrians jumping out the way as he rode with no respect for anyone in front of him or himself, lost in a mental hole no thoughts just actions, a moment of space for Dan who's mind was normally filled with thoughts and questions.

As Dan rode between two cars skimming the mirrors with his bars, he saw the sign for the harbour, the boat is close, the boat is waiting, he thought; *'We can make it, we can escape leave all this mess behind and free ourselves from the shackles of our life and our fucked up history we carry. This is the moment we start over the moment we are reborn.'*

As the helicopter circled above the enraged officer shouted orders into her radio;

"Do not let him pass this time, your order is stop him at all cost!"

The officer felt the pressure of losing him, not able to directly be on the ground, trusting her staff to 'step up' and have the same commitment to stopping Dan as she did. The operation to stop him is poised, the police with spiked stingers ready to deploy and literally bring the trio of Dan, Joanne and his bike down, nobody could escape on a bike with flat tyres, the police vehicles all positioned funnelling him towards the 'sting' the group behind led by Blockhead trying to keep up, trying to keep Dan in sight, but only just able to keep up with his wild style riding. Nobody could keep up with a man who has no fear or respect of death, hurtling straight into its jaws.

As the 4x4 sat waiting for them, having managed to get in front of them while they tangled with the 'suited man', she sat with her engine running, looking at the police all positioned, taking up her front row seat to watch Dan's demise. The glee in her face was obvious as she waited to see him come to his end, clutching the picture of Billy in her hand she sent him a photograph of the police waiting for Dan with the phrase underneath the picture *'You will be avenged, he will pay dearly.'* Sitting with her smile large and her eyes wide, she looked like a kid waiting for Christmas day. Her excitement bubbled over, hoping that the police would accidentally kill him. Her smile remained as she imagined Dan crashing and hitting the wall, him and that floozy splattered on the ground. She rested her phone on the dashboard against the window, waiting to record as Dan came to meet his end.

CHAPTER 11:

THE END OF THE LINE

As Dan fiercely rounded the corner he saw Poole Bridge. A lifting bridge that allows the ships into the harbour, the police officer screamed into the radio;

"RAISE THAT FUCKING BRIDGE, WHY IS THAT BRIDGE NOT RAISED?!"

Blockhead and the group rode at the police cars and bikes, trying to draw them away, trying to tempt them to focus on them and clear a path for Dan, but nobody was interested, they only wanted Dan the orders were to stop him, the rest are just followers!

As the beast in Dan rose out of his deep sea of pain, he bore the mark of evil, the beast that gave him his power to always stride on, sat on his black throne, his blacked heart beat slowly, no three-figure heartbeat just a stillness, a calmness, a moment of clarity, revealing his life choices the darkness coming for him, surely those who despise their mother and father will be put to death! He thought to himself; *I have opened a door that cannot be closed and the fire burns from that door! I am both the Alpha and the Omega, I am the start and the end, dark and light, love and hate!'*

The police barricade was blocking Dan's Path as he sat on his vibrating dreams, staring down the barrel of the police blockade, trapped with his wings clipped ending his freedom flight and chance of utopia. Blockhead and the rest slowed as the realised the police have not chased them, as they turned and looked they see the police sat staring at Dan, with Dan and Joanne sat motionless and the bike alive, the noise from the exhaust resonating around like a drum beat adding its own sense of presence to the moment.

Dan looked down at his beautiful friend, who had led him from the shadows many times, resting his hand on the engine he spoke to the bike;

"Tell me your secrets oh wise master, teach me your vibrating language, show me the way and the light, teach me my direction lead me to my paradise away from this vile life of sadness, you are the only constant reliable thing I have ever had in my life, always there always caring always delighting me and giving me life"

Dan took a deep breath and looked over his shoulder;

"Joanne are you sure about this? Are you with me?"

Looking at Dan in his open face helmet, the flashing blue lights reflecting in his mirrored aviators, his beard blowing in the wind and his mouth tight, strong, defiant and in charge of his mind, the clarity was clear in his face and Joanne's confidence in Dan even stronger;

"Yes! You live we live, you die we die.....it's both of us or neither of us....save us or kill us either way you have me at your back as one, run for the sun carry me away, take me to tomorrow"

He turned to look at the police and picked his spot, storming forward in a swirl of noise and dust, the leaves from the trees flicked up off the road floating slowly back down as the trio loomed down the road towards the bridge at full throttle straight at the police, the sun setting on the horizon and casting a dark yellow hue to the sky.

Descending on the road block he flicked the bike to the left, drawing the police officers to one side as they position to try and stop him, they all stood firm with cars parked in front of them, a protective barrier to Dan, with strategic gaps ready to deploy the police stingers and bring him down. Dan's attitude was manic, no feelings other than the mania driving him hard with no thought or fears, full of confidence like an 80's rock star with a head full of coke, in his last few determined seconds the smallest reality of the situation poked through his confidence; *'This is it this is the day I die. I never actually finished my life, yet here is where it ends!'* Joanne's face defiant, she accepted this could be her end as Dan bellowed out his loud, deep voice.

"A man's gotta do what a man's gotta do. If you want out now's the time if you want in hold on!"

Joanne could not here anything he said but she was in, she was in alright, the most fearless she had ever been with her mind a strange contented stillness.

Dan forced the huge weight of his bike right, the rear wheel no longer holding full grip, sliding to the side leaning the bike further than he should he got between the white barrier on the kerb and parked police car, his handle bar clipped the rear of car and the bars were flung to the side as he tried to squeeze between them, the bars leaving a deep gouge in the back of the police car, paint flaked on to the ground, scraping the bar end caused the bike to wobble uncontrollably, a tank slapper on a huge bike. Grappling with the bike to pull it straight he did what any rider would, he grabbed a fist full of throttle, hoping for the best as he pointed the bike straight at the bridge, the bike reacting, feeling like a moody mare of a horse, trying to shake them off.

The orders to lift the bridge have been listened to, the barriers were dropping in front of the bridge and as Dan rode through the siren sounds, it's wail loud and obnoxious, warning of the bridge rising, the noise deafening them both and the red flashing lights almost hypnotising and reflecting off the mirrored aviators resting above his swollen bloody nose, screaming 'Bring me Valhalla!' His coffee stained teeth shown in full battle cry with a mix of dried blood and saliva being spat out as he shouted his Viking rant;

"Death in battle is glory, bring me Valhalla!"

Joanne stared over the shoulder of her love and fear with no emotion or visible fear from Dan just power. As the barrier dropped the lower hanging white mesh hit Dan in the face, he did not duck, he did not lower his head, he protected his pillion princess as he held his chin high, gritted his teeth and as he smashed through the lower part of the barrier, his already swollen face took the blow, splitting the semi healed nose, the pain not allowed into his mind, the adrenaline and three-figure heartbeat keeping it all in control, his aviator mirrored lenses cracked and the frame dug in to his face, sending blood splattering all over his face, beard and over his shoulder on to Joanne, her eyes wide and wild, she didn't even notice the blood, she had the 1000 yard stare a slow feeling taking over her in the pandemonium of fear.

The barrier came to its final resting place missing the lower guard, now shattered on the road, debris of white flung up in to the air and now behind them, the siren louder and the old square bridge starting to raise, it was clear a bike of this size could not jump the bridge, a moment of indecision, the bike could only make a small drop, go or stop, stop or go? In the time it has taken Dan to decide the bridge is now too high, no way can this threesome of delight make it now.

Indy looked on blocked by the police, her hands over her mouth the tears already running down her cheeks, Blockhead stern and staring, the rest with their heads dropped low, avoiding the image of their friend's demise fearing the worst and praying for the best. Emily muttered;

"I said no good would come of this"

Her faithful husband nodding knowing she was right as he listened to the sirens blaring out he prayed to himself;

"This is the modern bell tolling for Dan the time is now, the time has ended our friend is no more!"

Dan locked his rear wheel, sliding the bike, fighting to keep it upright as the bridge slowly raised, all Dan could see now is sky as the bridge slowly raised, with the incline now above 20 degrees, for the first time in his life he actually felt there is no way out, he could not take them over the edge, not with Joanne on the back, his love had made him save them all, without her he would have walked in the halls of the brave, standing shoulder to shoulder with his brave brothers and sisters, as he had no care for his own life and would of pinned the throttle and jumped the bridge looking for the Valkyries to carry him away.

The bridge was still slowly creeping its way towards the sky, with a large group of onlookers waiting for Dan to roll backwards and tumble down the bridge to the awaiting police, camera phones galore as the baying crowd wanted the social media glorified death of Dan to boost their own profiles. With a loud smoky start shaking the floor as it lurched into life, the 4x4 sped towards the barrier, the lone female driver with her phone wedged against the screen recording, the interior full of rubbish and half eaten food, her face contorted by her grief, anguish and hatred, unable to see clearly through the tears. With her foot firmly planted on the accelerator the vehicle bashed its way through the police cars, tossing them against the black posts, tearing across the stinger puncturing all the tyres, as she burst through, she sent the whole barrier splintering in to the air.

Powering the 4x4 up the raising bridge, the operative at the bridge control hit the emergency stop button pausing the it in mid-air, as she raged up the bridge with her tyres deflating and bulging she had one aim and one aim alone, death to Dan as she slammed on the brakes, her deflated tyres were nearly pulled off the rims, the vehicle sliding sideways out of control, the side of the vehicle hitting Dan's bike and throwing the trio forwards off the bridge, the gasps from the onlookers were in unison, heard over the raucous noise of the bike taking Dan and Joanne to their watery death. The 4x4 with two wheels hanging over the bridge was teetering towards its own watery grave, an instant regret inside the 4x4 as she burst into a wail of tears, fearing for her life and regretting the feeling she was left with, the feeling of being a killer!

The orders from the police in the helicopter now getting more and more fraught;

"Leave that psychopath in the 4x4! Get me Dan, bring me his head on a platter but get me that wayward biker!"

The police, medics and fire crews on the ground looking blankly at each other, no way have either of them survived that fall, if they did they will now drown before we can get to them, the first commanding officers of the crews all now group together, one by one they turned down the lunatic in charge on the radio, who is now bellowing orders to leave a stranded live woman hanging over a bridge to search for a couple of dead bodies. With a plan in place the fire crew drive the fire truck up to the base of the bridge sending out the ladder to the stranded vehicle, police now stopping the media getting to close and the ambulance crew poised waiting for her to be brought down from her precarious position.

As the hero of the moment tracked his way along the outstretched ladder, step by step slowly and precisely following all of his training, his 20 years of service and most of all his gut instinct serving him well, the most important part of him is the fireman himself, risking his life to save another, no questions, no second thoughts just doing his job, but ignoring the radio orders from above.

The female officer in the helicopter was now literally bouncing around with rage screaming at the pilot to get her on the ground;

"Get me to that fucking water; get me on the fucking ground now!"

The helicopter pilot, a mid-forties family man with wayfarer sunglasses and a helmet bearing the name Pegasus written on it, coupled with a picture of the Greek horse next to it. Slowly and calmly he turned his head slightly back and in a well-spoken accent gave her an ultimatum;

"If you don't return to the your seat we will all end up on the ground much faster than we would like, when you have buckled up and buttoned that mouth I will land this big bird on the ground where I see fit and when I see fit, in this helicopter I am in charge, not the police"

Her enraged face tight lips and clenched hands all now communicating louder than she had screamed;

"I have told you sit in your seat and buckle up or I return to base."

Slamming herself in to the seat and snatching at the belt her hands still red for being   clenched so hard, she tossed her mic and headphones to the side and glared at the pilot, who simply and gently coasted the helicopter down towards a field several hundred feet away from the water.

As he brought the helicopter down he chuckled to himself;

"I hope you have enjoyed your flight we look forward to seeing you again"

Fortunately the officer did not hear him, even if she had he held all the power and he knew it, the smugness of the pilot so obvious and so loud his cheesy grin was enough to let her know how much he enjoyed giving her orders.

As the helicopter neared the ground she thought about all the people Dan had chasing him, the ones who wanted to stop him, the man who swung from a tree no longer alive, the man in the limousine no longer alive and the woman in the 4x4 balancing with the grim reaper on the bridge.

"Only I can stop him only I can bring him down, he better not be dead I want him, I want to be the one to wipe that smile of his face and bring him to my world, a world he will wish he never entered!"

On the opposite side of the water a lone man was sitting on his custom sidecar and motorbike, the loving shed built bike, caressed and loved so many times as Dan and Morris worked on it through the years. Morris took off his helmet, and looked for any sign off Dan. The water was fast and flowing well, the tide changing, the tears were already welling in the eyes of an old, sorry man, a man who has missed his chance to redeem himself for both Dan and Dotty. The gut-wrenching pain engulfed him, his brow furrowed and his throat burned, swallowing hard, fighting back the horrid feeling of self-loathing, failure and sorrow, thinking;

I am too late, I have killed him I have caused this I should have been here to help him the last few years, he needed me and I let him down, worse I let Dotty down and for that I cannot bear', his face was showing his failure and the tears showed his sorrow, a broken man distraught past the point of no return, a man on the edge with nothing to live for and nothing to gain by living.

As the 4 x4 teeters on the edge of the bridge the group sat on their bikes in horror, having followed Dan hundreds of miles since he wandered into their lives and rippled revelations through it. The pained faces of all were tearing through them and cutting them to the core. They are dead! The thought struck the group cold Emily was crying with her head hung low, arms still wrapped around her man, whimpering, *He really is gone.* Blockhead stern and strong with his eyes narrow, swallowing his pain and swallowing his grief, clenching his teeth together pain in his jaw controlling his emotions. Richie revved his super single motor hard, the slow thumping a raucous noise drowning out his sorrow. The real pain touched Indy, a beautiful fresh flower stricken with the grief of loss, the loss of Dan and the loss of herself.

The torture of what she did in that petrol station still splattered on her rear wheel the very make up of her hippy free love mind crumbled and in ruin, she is a killer and that fact hardened her and destroyed her, gone is her free spirited care free nature replaced with a trauma and a developing neurosis.

Indy was now an eagle with a broken wing, spiralling out of control and heading for a crash.

As her broken mind crumbled she turned the key of her bike, she ripped off the fluffy pink keyring and threw it over her shoulder no longer is she a fluffy pink type, now she is hollow and dark, placed on a path of revelations tracking towards Dan's road of despair. The V twin rumble vibrated in the frame, shaking the bike, rattling the fixings and shaking the long chopper forks, as she slowly rode away she turned her head away from the group unable to look at them, no connection with any of them or herself, slowly the rain of pain in her head which was tormenting her grew heavy and her head of hope now gone and as low as the sun, which as it dropped was turning the sky a deep red hue. Indy wanted no more from them, she had no idea what she wanted; only that she could not stay and watch them pull Dan's dead body out of the water.

As Indy's bike trundled away her tears rolled down her face, her happiness literally draining from her with every salty tear, she no longer saw herself as the ray of sunshine who only brought happiness, she is a murderer, a killer a vile person who brought pain on another person, even though she knew she did it to save Dan, she cannot forgive herself for a cold blooded attack, one so brutal, one so aggressive. She is not the woman she thought she was.

Her beloved bike carried her away, but drags behind it a dirty secret, the evidence plastered over the back of the bike. The torment her mind gave her more than the pain of death, like a martyr she embraced the pain, almost encouraging it to take hold of her. 'I deserve pain I deserve punishment, I despise who I am, never will I be able to smile again, I don't deserve happiness or redemption only pain'.

The darkness started to fall, shrouding the moment but hiding nothing as Benjie got off his bike he blew a kiss to his wife, standing proud and solid, an old man full of experience and life having lived through many a hardship, he had never dropped his faith in himself or his wife. In a slow low voice he started his prayer;

"Our father who art in Valhalla

Freedom be thy name

Thy warriors come

Thy wisdom will be done

On soil as it is in Asgard

Give us this sunset our journey to you

As we face up to our failings

And forgive others of their failings

Lead us in to the great hall of glory

Deliver us to our forefathers

For thine is the truth

In death and honour

For ever standing in the hall of the great warriors

Amen"

The moment was beautiful and fitting as they mourned the loss of their great warrior, taken by the Valkyries to Odin himself, to be honoured as a great man should, standing high in the clouds to be emulated and respected by all.

As he got back on his bike his wife nodded with her eyes full of tears and her heart singing the words that she has just heard from the love of her life;

"Benjie that was beautiful a true hero's prayer you are my hero and always will be, he leans in whispers to her you are my everything you always have been and even Odin himself could not change that!

As the prayer of Odin floats off with the Valkyries on the other side of the water the shattered heart of Morris screamed the pain up his spine and into his head, louder than anything he has ever heard before, draped across his tank nothing left in his soul, emptied of life beaten to the very end of his existence no fight or flight just the pain of failure over Dan and the loss of his wife eating away at every part of his mind.

As he lay forward on to his bike unable to fight back at the pain, a faint voice whistled through the air to him.

"Morris Morris. Help, please help me please. Daaaaaaaad."

CHAPTER 12:

MY SAVIOUR

Morris lifted his head up in disbelief; *'I must be hearing things! Surely not.'* Morris was discretely parked down a little side road, his bike ridden all the way down to the quayside with boats moored against the jetty, the 4x4 balanced precariously, in view above the roof tops on the top of the raised bridge and a lone fireman extended on a ladder trying to get her out. The blue lights of the fire engine constantly illuminated the quay as they flashed on and off, the smell of the fishing boats rank and decayed, the dark shroud as the light drops, with the setting sun making it hard to see any detail. Morris thought; *'Is it Dan is Dan still alive?'*

As he jumped from his motorbike and ran to the edge he saw Dan clinging to the jetty by one arm and the other wrapped around his love, his new life, Joanne had her arms wrapped tightly around Dan and her head pushed hard against his chest, shivering and crying, Dan struggling to keep them from drowning, partially out of the water holding their lives in the one handed grip he had on the wet mooring rope running down the jetty post. Morris dropped to his knees grabbing at Dan's soaked leather Jacket, trying to pull them up but as he tried with all his strength he could not lift them up. Even as a young, strong man this would have been an impossible task, a small pained smile crept over Dan's face. He had known it was Morris, as Dan had hung from the rope losing all hope of survival, he had recognised the sound of Morris' bike approaching he knew it better than his real father's voice.

Morris jumped to his feet with the speed of a man in his 20's, ignoring all the pains of an old man as he runs to the bike, Dan's weak voice creeping along the Jetty.

"Daaaaaadd please don't leave me we need you"

A man on a mission, not hearing only doing, the side car was kitted out for every eventuality, with a shovel, ropes, plus hidden away a revolver from WW2 and a sawn-off shot gun tucked in a secret side compartment with lots of ammunition. Throwing the rope around the back of the side car outfit, he ran back to Dan and Joanne dropping to his painful old knees, looping the old rope under Dan's arms;

"This is not going to be pleasant but it's all we got son"

With a couple of kicks the old English parallel twin burst into life, slowly he let the clutch out and gently feathered it with the throttle, pulling them slowly, trying to not hurt them, as Dan's helmet loomed up above the jetty he softened the throttle and slipped the clutch, drawing them up as gentle can be done but still the edge of the jetty scraped at his back, ripping at his skin through the wet leather, the pain excruciating but he swallowed hard and tightened his grip on Joanne, he clenched his teeth and grimaced in pain;

"I got you babe"

She felt safe yet scared, the water having frozen her skin and stripped her of all strength, clinging to Dan her eyes tightly shut and her body shivering. Morris 'killed the engine' and grabbed the hand gun, stuffing it in his trouser pocket as he ran over to them;

"Come on you don't have any time, get up get up"

Dan whispered into her ear;

"Come on princess we have to run, I have got this but you need to get up"

Her fingers were so cold she could barely move them, Morris peeled her from Dan and tried to get her walking, her legs buckled as she tried to walk, Dan was fighting back his own pain scooping her up in his arms, trying not to roar in pain himself, as he gently and painfully leaned forward to place her in the side car, Morris grabbed his arm;

"There is a place you can go, here is the address I have lived there far too long when I should have been here with you, I owe them a favour as they were so good to me but go, tell them I sent you and you are my son, they will help you"

Dan literally bust in to tears crying like he had never cried before;

"You are my dad and always will be"

He threw his soaked arms around Morris and hugged him with a lifetime of love;

"Thank you Dad I love you"

The words poured out with his tears, washing away so much old pain as he stood dripping on the wooden jetty.

"Give me your jacket and helmet there is more dry clothes in my in the side car get yourself across the channel and go to that address, I will take care of things here, no buts no discussion save your lady before it's too late!"

A moment of silence that felt like hours, as he looked at the old English bike the pair of them had built together he knew they would always be together, that bike was them. As he jumped on to the bike grabbing the old helmet from the seat , he pulled the blanket from between the bungees on the back of the side car, even in his rush he still made time to place the blanket neatly over Joanne, tucking it in around her to keep her warm she opened one eye and the moment pauses, the world stopped spinning, their love felt deep and strong and with one strong wink and a defiant look on his battered pained face, he kicked the kick start and the bike started on the first attempt, the memories of years gone by building this bike and sometimes just sitting with a mug of tea in the shed, just chatting and looking at the simplistic beauty of it flooded in to his mind, warming him from the soul outwards, he looked over his shoulder to see Morris stood saluting him with the hand gun pointed to his head.

"Daaaaadd nooooooooo"

The wail cut the air sharply, Morris was stood in Dan's helmet and jacket on the edge of the Jetty.

"Dan goooo save your love, save her I am finished I have nothing left you are me, live out my dreams and love her like I loved Dotty, make me proud"

Dan edged the bike down the narrow access road, as he passed the rusty corrugated steel structures, a modern 'sat nav' bolted to the old bars reads Dee way turn left the end of the road, he took one last look over his shoulder as a light illuminated the whole quay he was just on, a loud female amplified voice shouted;

"Put down your weapon, this in the police!"

The coast guard boat was turning the corner to the quay they had been stood on;

"I repeat. Put down your weapon!"

Dan stopped the bike to see Morris facing him he moved the gun downwards and pointed the gun to his chest; he pulled the trigger firing a bullet in to his heart, a heart broken and empty since Dotty had been taken from him all those years ago. The moment slowed as Morris started to fall backwards wearing Dan's Helmet and Jacket, a feeling of happiness and love ripped from Dan's chest as he watched Morris drop in to the water.

As his body slowly sunk into the cold dark watery grave, the emotions fell with him, Morris had nothing left and in his last ditch attempt to save Dan, the shot to his heart did not pain him, did not scare him and did not kill him as he was going to meet Dotty and join her in everlasting love. He knew his love was waiting for him, without her he had struggled and his heart empty the only thing he wanted was to dance with her again, showing his love to the only woman for him. Morris had a strangled love in his heart stood on the quay, but knew Dan needed time and a distraction from the police causing them to not be looking for him. The old soul sunk into the water with a euphoric feeling taking over from the pain, the water rippled and bubbled as the body slowly slipped into the darkness.

The spirt of Morris floated above the quay and Dotty danced into his arms they skipped across the water like time had never been interrupted, the dance of two lost lovers whole again, riding their way to eternity. Dan's moment was a polar opposite, grief stricken, forced to remember the day his dad killed himself and his mother, the tears fell like a waterfall and the pain made his entire body shake, the gut wrenching knot in his stomach tearing his internals like his broken heart. Not many people witness two fathers shoot themselves and this time he experienced both at once. Looking down at Joanne he tries to gather his broken mind together he thought, '*I need to make this right I need to make a family I need to make this right!*'

As the sidecar rounded the bend he passed the new lifting sail bridge, where was he going, he needed Jack's boat, where would it be? Jack had said sail from the sail and meet with the royal Aphrodite. The thoughts of the cryptic words Jack had left him at the side of the road, now bent his already distorted mind, the grief tumbling around inside his head, splitting straight through tortured thoughts.

As he carried his love in the sidecar, trying to remaster the skills of an old outfit, the sail bridge was now behind him, had he missed the boat? As he looked up the royal sign of the lifeboats loomed into view above the tree line. Royal this has to be it! Grabbing a fist full of brakes the sidecar with his all his love sat on his right tried to continue forward, turning the bike violently left as it tried to overtake them, pointing the bike down the side of the lifeboat college, fighting with the sidecar outfit knowing his skills are 'rusty' and this is his only chance at happiness, he snaked the bike down a small road with many small boats stood up against the wall. As he got to end of the narrow road a boat illuminated, blinding him startling him and terrifying him, the rear of the ferry was backed up with the rear open and written on the boat, '*Aphrodite Goddess of the Sea*'. This was it.

Dan apprehensively approached the open boat and a large gun appeared in front of them, held by an even larger man;

"*Halt*"

The word stern and forceful, Dan lifted his head up as the man pushed the gun in to Dan's chest;

"You look like you have had a rough night, but this ain't your boat"

Dan tried to stay strong, but in a quivered scared voice;

"Jack sent me, Jack said I should cross as him, Jack said this is my escape sail from the sail"

The man reached for his phone, the pressure from the gun burning into the chest of a once strong man now at a desperate end. As the gun dropped the light from the boat is still blinding;

n*"Get on. Captain says you are on!"*

As Dan rides the bike onto the boat the inside is stacked with supplies and weaponry, a row of bikes was strapped to the floor, a man sat with his feet up on his girder forks puffing away on a huge cigar;

"Dan I didn't think you were going to make it"

The confusion spiralled around Dan's head, what who Jack?

"You fuckin made it man I thought you were a goner when you took a swim, that old man had your back when he dragged you out the water alright"

Dan immediately burst into tears, tears of joy to be on the boat tears of joy to have Joanne safe, tears of pain as Morris was gone for good. Jack slowly walked across to him and placed a hand on his shoulder;

"You have had a tough time my friend here you need this more than me!"

Jack passed him a hip flask of Whiskey. Dan sipped at the teat of escapism once more, it was going to take more than this flask to repair tonight, he gently slid one hand under the blanket, his quivering dirty hand linked into Joanne's hand like only lovers could;

"We made it Joanne, we are free"

Jack signalled to the rear of the boat and the door slowly closed;

"You two come up when you are ready, you're safe here and we will be in France tomorrow"

Dan dropped down into the sidecar wrapping him arms around Joanne;

"I am sorry"

She looked up at his bloody face and tried to smile;

"Well that was exciting"

With that she snuggled into him, their love making them one.

The boat gently moved away and the motion cradled them both in the sidecar, in love just where Morris and Dotty had spent many of their early days. As they both now lay in each other's arms, still damp and with the stench are the sea filling their nostrils, the feeling of trepidation was strong;

"Where next Mr lone wolf? Where next?"

Dan reached in to his pocket and pulled out the address Morris had given him;

"We have a place of sanctuary but first we need to get there"

He leaned forward and typed the address in to the GPS and the route calculated 750 Miles, his heart sunk at the thought of another full day of riding. As he looked back at Joanne;

"It's not far princess, I will take us to safety"

As they lay cuddled in the side car the gentle rocking of the boat allowed them to drift away from the sea fairing stench and the collected decades of musty damp smells in the sidecar that cradled them, rocking back and forth they fell asleep in a moment of clarity, a moment of togetherness and sanctuary from the pandemonium of grief outside.

The body of Morris sank deeper into the water, the coast guard boat docked and requested a diving team to recover him, nothing like this was ever fast but the lead officer was pacing and screaming;

"Get him out that water, get him on this boat, where are the blue light brigade? Get one of them in there to fish him out"

The boat had stopped at the small dock where Morris had shot himself, a small dimly lit dock with an untidy appearance and a smell that was overpowering; this was clearly an old small fishing boat area.

As the lead officer got off the boat she hurriedly dropped to the ground leaning over the edge looking for any sign of life, nothing but dark putrid water an unfitting grave for a man as noble as Morris, looking further out with her torch the radio crackled in to life;

"Watch manger Waldron Victor Zero One, priority message, one female casualty rescued from the vehicle on the bridge using extrication equipment. Police assistance required for fire and ambulance crew safety, as casualty is presenting aggressively and may require physical restraint. Victor Zero One over"

Her face screwed up, anger and frustration bubbling over under her own stress;

"What are uniform doing, why aren't they helping? Get them pricks over there to sort her out, then bring her cuffed to me, let's find out who she is."

Shaking her head in disgust she mumbled;

"Dan this is not over, dead or alive this is not over!"

As a marked police car screeches up on to the dock.

"You're needed over the water; the woman they rescued is going crazy"

The look of content slaps at the officer as she screws up her nose.

"That's Ms Blackstone to you and why can uniform not deal with it!"

Strutting towards the uniformed officers with a walk of woman on a mission, the strides hard long and fierce, the expression of a solider going into battle;

"Tania we have her in the back of the van, she is going mental are you sure you want to interview her now?"

Tania had been a lead officer for many years, worked her way up the ranks from the bottom, she had struggled her way to the top and had no time for fools. A woman hardened by personal and professional life and it showed all over her face, the uniformed officer backed away slowly from the glare alone that Tania threw at the uniformed officer. Her mind raging and her temper short, her reputation is even fiercer than her facial expressions and the reality off her much worse than her reputation. More stories had been told about her closed door custody interrogations than Wyatt Earp, she had been threatened with dismissal more times that she has years of service, but she always got the job done, taking no grief from senior officers or the criminals she interrogates.

She opened the rear door of the police van, the rescued driver was cuffed and sat on the seat, the glares between the two were like fire and ice, a meeting of two hardened women, one smart and dressed in power looking into the eyes of an old strong scruffy cuffed woman. The few silent seconds between them showing the force of their intentions and the harshness they carry.

Tania stepped in to the van power suited but no jewellery with standard issue police boots on, a smart woman who would literally kick ass if she needed, no pretty delicate shoes in sight just the reek of power hungry corruption. As Tania looked over her shoulder the uniformed officers know, they close the door and walk away. She slowly returned her gaze to the scruffy woman slouched in her seat;

"I don't have time for long life stories, you have two minutes to tell me why you rammed that bike over the edge and where the fuck you came from, if you don't tell me in two minutes I will back this van up to the doc, ram you out in to the fucking water and see how far you get in them cuffs! I know you have followed him a long way I have seen your crazy antics and your lunatic driving, now let's start with why?"

The crazy look in the cuffed woman's eyes fades, replaced with sadness and a disappointment, her strength slipping away and her grief poking through. Tania had no time for tears or emotion no care for her as a person she just wanted answers, the woman struggled to pull some paper from her breast pocket, Tania rolled her eyes;

"Don't you fucking cry on me, just spit it out!"

As the woman pulled out a newspaper clipping, she looked up with her eyes full of tears, the grief of Billy coupled now with the remorse of murder, her hands shaking as she offered the clipping up towards the 'carbon lady' a strong and precise woman with a single focus, she took the clipping and carefully unfolded it.

The clipping was well used and tatty and so were the two photographs loosely kept inside the folded up paper, her analytical mind in over drive she looked at a her prisoner, a quizzical look as she glanced back down to the pictures, a picture of a man and a woman at a dinner somewhere, happy relatively well dressed and strong body language, it is the same scruffy woman but the strength has gone and the years have aged her, the other picture a burned man slumped in his chair with his dog. 'The carbon Lady' knew Dan's files inside out, she now knew who these people are and what Dan did, she had studied it as part of her degree in law. She nodded turned and left the van;

"Get her to the cells, get her cleaned up and look after her I will be back to interview her"

The police officers looked in seeing no blood, no beating nothing, in a shocked moment unable to comprehended what Tania had said, one muttered;

"Did she ask us to look after someone? That's a turn up for the books; normally we are trying to cover up for her"

The radio crackled again;

"You need to see this Tania. He is really old I though Dan was in his 50's not his 70's"

Shaking her head and looking along the estuary not a moving boat to be seen;

"Get that fucking helicopter back!"

She stood with a helpless rage vibrating though her body she had never failed to make her arrest, the torture of the situation pinching her brow and paining her head; she knew Dan is somewhere out there, but where?

The pain in Dan's head tried to make sense of why Morris, a man he worshiped killed himself the same way a man he hated did, the confusion was too much to bear he lay there crying like a baby with the years of grief stabbing at him, hurting his entire mind body and soul. Cradled in his arms the only chance of love resting on his chest. She looked up at him not even able to imagine why or what has just happened, looking for any words that might help;

"He has saved us, set us free we owe him, we owe him to start again and live his dreams"

She carefully brushed away his tears, he was more vulnerable now than he had ever been, possibly more broken than she could ever imagine and he was unable to muster any words, barely able to keep himself together his lips quivering his face contorted a small nod was all he could give her right now and she understood, lowering her head onto his chest and settling down, Dan hasn't pushed her away yet and in his grief he is one false move from wanting a solitary life, away from everyone, protecting himself from the herds of people including Joanne.

As the boat gently sailed they were rocked to sleep again drifting back into an escape from the tortured place they had found themselves in, Jack shouted suddenly down from the deck;

"We are about to dock, get yourself ready, we will not have time to sightsee!"

CHAPTER 13:

RUNNING FOR A NEW LIFE

As the boat docked it was all hands on deck, people came from everywhere, some packing the bikes, some loading bags, tossing them to others to load onto the bikes, the general noise of people running around above deck creating a frantic buzz. Clearly there was no time to hang around and as Dan pushed the side car outfit backwards and Joanne tried to help;

"No darling. Rest, relax and get ready to leave, I have no idea what this will be like."

As she sunk back down into the sidecar she pulled the blanket around herself, her knee knocked against the top of the sidecar causing a flap to fall open. With a sharp intake of breath she felt an uncontrollable fear, a gun had been stowed away with boxes of ammunition staring at her. The hum drum life was dull but this exciting life was getting far more risky than she ever imagined it could be.

As the bike kicked over and spluttered into life the gun rattled in its holder, she pushed the flap closed and looked up at Dan, catching the pain in his eyes before he turned away to avoid her looking into his painful heart, the gun had terrorised his emotions drawing him back to heartaches new and old. The surrounding havoc calms as man joins machine all sat on their metal steeds, no joviality but a job to be done. Jack loomed into view, taking his position on his bike at the back; one by one they all started their bikes. The smallest ray of light started to appear through the top of the ship door, the whirring of the door drowned out by the noise of the bikes engines running vibrating and chugging along almost melodic, raging and ready to rampage. Jack pulled his bike up against Dan;

"You're welcome to stick with us and we will shield you, I don't think you should be riding alone, you need protection"

The words bounced off Dan's shield of pain, as he hid himself from everything, fear love or any emotion even the offer of solidarity and protection from a man he respected.

The further the door lowered the more of the dim morning light peaked through, the small early sunlight stirring the desire to ride, a desire to escape the sorrow and outrun the problems in his head, the hope gently scratched at Dan but barely made any indent into his cold darkened mind. Dan knew he had been in this mental place before but never as dark, never as cold and never as painful as this. This road would be long and Dan's mind needed a primeval escape to lose himself in.

Unsure when and how he would be able to shed this blanket of darkness draped around his shoulders, one that weighed him down more than he thought possible, the sinking feeling was worse than ever with his hope lost and the darkness growing in him, turning down the sunlight to a dim dark dull light as it slowly engulfed the boat with the door now nearly fully open, the other riders putting on a range of different sunglasses, the older guys using aviators, the younger guys in wayfarers and Jack with a large cigar puffing away at the back, the sense of occasion high, the stirring of adventure and excitement.

The door clanged against the landing dock with an eerie echo ringing around the boat, the noise reverberating across the floor and shaking the bikes, Joanne sinking further into the sidecar and hiding herself away, the noise of the door overshadowed by the revving of the bikes as they exited the boat, leaving a cloud of dust and they ride out, two bikes at a time leave side by side. As Dan looked at Jack the mutual understanding of two warriors was obvious, two men fighting different battles for different causes but a connection of respect and morals holding them in the same moment, as Jack leaned forward he placed a hand on the shoulder of Dan, the feeling barely registered into his stony feelings;

"You are always welcome at my door, in triumph or tribulations I will always be here for you you're my brother and an equal, may our lives join again"

Before the words could sink into his mind, Jack was gone, tearing after his brotherhood life, one that meant more to him than his own life.

Slowly but confidently Dan followed the path laid in the dust and dirt by the brotherhood, the morning light making him squint, with no real idea of what lay in front of them he looked at the 'sat nav' as it 'kicks' into life; *'turn left in 1.1 miles, 713 miles to destination'*, the ride to the address Morris had given him was such a long way but if Morris said that's where they should go that is where they should go. The feelings of worry crept in to his head and ate away at his spirit, his hope and positivity already broken, now crushed by the thought of this journey, with nothing to inspire him but the thought of fulfilling the last wishes of dear old Morris, but 700 miles with no money or food was not going to work, the tank on this bike would only give about 95 miles with the chair attached and Dan's stomach would only give him about 50 miles before his hunger would begin to taunt him.

The miles clicked by and the thoughts in his mind assaulted him, more and more miles rolled by and the sun shone but his view was dark and the scenery unseen, the flora and fauna not even registering, just a green and grey surround, the beauty of the scenery lost. The only care he had was resting under the blanket next to him, how he wished things were different so very different, partying at the bike rally rather than battling with the grief and regret he carried, battling on against his own mood and the hurt, trying to make sense of Morris and his life. *'Why did he not come back sooner? Why did he leave me? Why did he kill himself?'* The road sweeping, rising and falling as it flowed across the French countryside, the darkness surrounding his view falls away as the road became the teacher and Dan its student.

The visceral and relaxed experience chipped away at the toughened mind-set that Dan had found himself in, creating a zen like feeling as the smells of the countryside started to seep into his nostrils, the sickness starting to subside as the world started to poke its way back into Dan's view.

With his mind starting to piece itself together again his thoughts turned to worries, this outfit had never reached 100 miles on one tank before and they were getting close to that now, with no money and no food the worries come thick and fast wave after wave of anxiety, *'What next how do we get through this? I don't want to steal I don't want to hurt anyone, how can I get us to safety with no money, I so wish Morris was here he would have had a plan'.*

Dan hated taking from others and could not bear to think he may be forced to steal money, food or fuel, screwing his face up, that's not who I am that's not what I do, but what else can I do?

As Dan expected the bike reached 85 miles on the trip counter and began to cough and splutter, the all too familiar lack of fuel. Dan reached down to the reserve switch, fumbling around. The switch wasn't there any more what had Morris done? Coasting the bike to the side of the road Dan got off the bike with Joanne silently worrying and wondering why they were stopping.

"I need to find the reserve tap, Morris must have relocated it"

As he looked around both sides of the bike, with nothing standing out to him the fear came into his mind with a feeling of them being a pair of 'sitting ducks', waiting to be caught.

Looking closer under the tank, Dan saw a modern switch and a fuel pump from an old car bolted under the right hand side;

"What has that crazy old fool been up to?"

Following the pipes down to the underside of the sidecar his shock made him gasp loudly literally taking a step back;

"What is it Dan?"

As Dan shook his head a large smile and a melancholy feeling washed over him, the hairs on his neck and arms stood up and he was in a lovely memory, a distant memory of a drawing he once saw on the shed wall. Morris had fitted a petrol tank from a car under the sidecar and the pump would fill the bike's tank.

"That crazy old man is a legend he has saved us there is a full tank of fuel here easily 700 ish miles worth, maybe even enough to get us to his place, he knew what he was doing."

Flicking the switch he heard the pump swirl into life, drawing up the sweet amber fuel filling the tank on the bike. Joanne started to rummage under the seat pulling out old newspapers and photographs, as she started to look through the old pictures, the vision of two lovers dancing their way through life flooded her mind, pictures of this very sidecar and bike in so many wonderful locations, clearly this was Dotty in the side car and Morris on the bike in amazing scenery and many picnics, stirring a warm feeling in Joanne with thoughts of a bygone era and a desire to emulate their love.

The pictures spanned many years and much happiness as she flicked from beautiful scene to beautiful scene, a small envelope fell from in between the pictures into her lap with 3 bold letters scribbled on to it; DAN.

Sitting in the sidecar wondering if to give it to Dan or not, she contemplated would this be good or bad inside? Would it be joy or sorrow? What should she do? Watching Dan escaping his pain as he fiddled with the bike, she knew that his bikes carried him to a safe place, the pump drawing fuel from the tank under her seat that vibrated the whole sidecar giving her a tingling feeling throughout her finger and toes;

"Dan this has your name on it"

The escape he had been safe in dropped away with a mental clang in his head, back in reality he recognised the shaky writing that was from Morris, his nose flared with a sharp exhale and the emotion flooded into his eyes so fast he could barely see. Nodding his head and taking the note a single tear rolled down his check, he turned his head away trying to hide it from her, but she saw it and she knew how much he was hurting.

The shaky writing on the oil and tea stained paper read:

Dan I am always with you even when I am not, you are me and I am you, this bike is us and Dotty all rolled into one and this bike will outlast us all. I am not sure how this will all pan out but if I am not there to see it, make it special and I will feel it. If you haven't figured it out yet you have lost your touch, there is a large tank and a pump connected to the new electronic reserve switch, with enough fuel in it to get you to my escape, go to the address I owe them a favour they saved me. Please look after Joanne like I wish I could have looked after Dotty. Live your dream and make it happen bring it to life!

I love you so much and would give you anything including my life!

P.s stay honest the small bag under the seat will help.

All my love Dad

With his face still turned away floods of tears soaking his beard his feet walking him backwards and forwards trying to keep himself together when two gentle arms slid around his waist, Joanne's gentle voice floated around his ears;

"We got this Dan"

His shoulders dropped and as he turned he cried into her shoulder, the letter bringing his emotions to their knees. He bearded cheek brushing her soft skin he mumbled;

"I love you and Morris has got this!"

Confused and emotional he strode off to the side car, her soft vulnerable yet hard man leaned into the sidecar, reaching under the seat he found the bag Morris mentioned in his note, as he pulled it felt attached to something. Now with his whole head in the sidecar under the seat he saw the bag cable tied to the seat runners, undoing the straps of the bag it released from the cable ties and out rolled bundles of money, Morris always had a plan and a way to prepare like no one else could, an ability to know what might be needed and set the wheels in motion.

The confused mental state of happiness and sorrow fighting the now familiar battle in his head, with handfuls of cash he stood holding the bundles up like an offering;

"I told you Morris got this"

Every word drew more emotion into his face, fighting the pain and trying to smile;

"The old man always had my back, even before I knew it"

Dan bundled the money into the bag and tossed it to Joanne;

"Come on princess time to head for the hills!"

The awkward smile not able to mask his sorrow but a smile it was nonetheless.

Roaring the beautiful old bike out of the dust fighting with the steering keeping it true, leaving some hurt behind to settle in the dirt, Dan carried hope in his heart and a special thought in his head; 'I want to be just like Morris.', little did he know he was already more like Morris than he could ever try to be, he had learned his morals and inner voice from Morris and gained his feistiness from Dotty, he was a product of them and one day he would realise how much like them he actually was.

The road brought the ever calm sanctuary to them both, the feeling of meditation and worship crept into their souls, the road was forever the teacher, the master and their deity. The signs started to show tourist France in the distance, Parc Naturel Régional des Boucles de la Seine Normande, but this was no sightseeing tour this was an escape, a run for life, a new start!

The constant beauty of the parallel twin engine purring and vibrating along was hypnotic, the pair now tiring and settling in to the monotony of the journey, the miles clicked along, there had been very few vehicles on this road but a set of lights had been in the mirrors for the last few miles, was this the police? Dan thought; 'Do I tell Joanne, do I just go hell for leather? Or just ride it out and see where it goes?'

The lights from behind gradually got closer, Dan feared he might not be able to outrun them with this old sidecar outfit, so he slows, thinking 'if I slow enough they will just overtake me and I will know it was just some random nobody going nowhere that I care'. With the lights close behind, sure enough the indicator comes on and a large old estate car started to overtake, the relief in Dan was huge, this old car would never be a police car, the windows were steamed up and the car filthy, the car was so close as it passed, creating that feeling of vulnerability, easing off the throttle slightly and allowing the outfit to slow, counter steering as the side car reacted against the bikes deceleration.

The large estate pulled in front of them and slammed on the brakes, the car already nearly in contact with the front of the sidecar, horror poured across Dan's face, the brakes on this old outfit nowhere near as good as the car in front, trying to keep the bike tracking straight the rear of the car makes contact and they are jolted forward, Dan now half sat on his tank and Joanne thrown half asleep against the front of the sidecar, the brakes of the estate car still on and forcing them to a stop, the glare of the red lights blinding them in a panic of red.

As Dan jumped off and charged at the car, the visions of the drunk driver back in England surged through Joanne's mind, the terror of Dan's rage ever present. Four men jumped out of the car with batons and in a strong French accent start to demand money passports and phones;

"English pigs give them now or we kill your lady in front of you"

The bigger of the French men spits on the floor repeating himself "English Pigs" Dan weary and tired, already beaten and battered, physically and mentally turns his back and walks back to his bike as he looks over his shoulder with gritted teeth;

"Fuck You"

The largest French man in full flight jumped on Dan's back yanking him down to the ground shouting;

"I will take your lady and show her a better time than you could ever do!"

They wrestled on the ground, he had no fight left and no strength, pinned on the road and now left with no options, about to lose everything including his dignity, the men started to walk over to Joanne still huddled in the side car, they giggled like school boys muttering in French as they step over to grab her, she flung the blanket that has been protecting her from the cold bitter wind upwards, the blanket shielding her from sight as it momentarily hangs tossed in the air, as it drops it reveals a woman with a 'no fucks attitude' one foot on the seat of the side car and one on the front of it holding Morris's gun in her hands.

She fired a bullet straight at the men who dived to the ground covering their heads; she turned to the man who is now lay partially across Dan;

"Get the fuck off him or I will fucking blow your mother fucking head off!"

The once 'large' man was running back to the car like a boy lost from his mum;

"Au revoir mother fuckers"

Dan dusted himself down looking at Joanne; the car wheel spun away throwing up dirt and debris as she fired a bullet straight in to the rear window, without even looking she popped more bullets in, as the gun snaped shut Dan jumped, the sight and sounds of the gun stirring up awful memories that danced like devils in his mind torturing him

"Don't look at me like that, a woman's gotta do what a woman's gotta do! It's not always the men that get to care of business, now get us the fuck out of here."

Slumping back into her seat with the gun stashed down the side of her legs;

"Morris took care of us he knew we might need this"

No words came back from a man grief-stricken trying to turn away the horrid memories he carries in his head. As the bike kicked over first time he remembered the legend of his old-school biker the one who inspired him, who he looked up to and the one that made him the man he was. Drawing the bike away back on to the road his torrid mind biting at him and fighting with him, slowly trying to destroy him, that part of the mind that is dark and self-loathing telling him, 'You are worthless, you should have protected her not lay in the dirt like a 'pussy'.

Joanne stared at the grief written all over him and climbed up on to the back of the bike to put her arms around him;

"We are a team we are one together, my success is your success and yours mine don't think I can't take care of myself or us, I just choose to let you normally"

With a large smile on her face she climbed back in to her chair, feeling like she was now equal, feeling she has grown and become one with Dan, knowing she was now ready for whatever life may bring, she stood proud with Dan by his side, an unstoppable force a team who are unbeatable, a couple who will be together forever.

As he looked down at the 'sat nav'; '559 miles to destination, 9hrs and 4 mins 'how long can I take this? It's unbearable I just want to be there now.' The miles drifted by so slowly, each mile a torrid argument with his own mind, reflecting and rationalising his way to survival the only way he knows how, but no revelations, no epiphany of delights just a battle in the dark clouded mind of a man who has never come to terms with any of his grief, carrying it around on his back dragging him down every time he struggled.

The borders came and went and the beauty of crossing a country lost, not seen not recognised by his shielded eyes, looking but not seeing, doing but not experiencing, closed off from a life that would hurt too much if he let it in right now. The worry of passport checks and borders brought a real fear for both of them, carrying an excess of fuel and a loaded gun; the slightest wrong move could start a search that would see them arrested in a country they did not really understand.

The fears and anxiety created a silence between them, a division and a void, trapped between past happiness and the unknown, the fear was real and the consequences of mistakes worse than the fears they had. The final border crossing did not cause any undue attention but they were not blending in with the norms and the herds of people, standing out loud and proud even though on this occasion Dan would for once wished to just blend in with the others and just drift into German countryside.

The police back in England had now informally identified Morris, the rage from Tania exploded across the room, kicking the door open;

"Get me on that fucking helicopter I need to be in France! He must have got on a boat!"

As Dan and Joanne drifted in to the last two hundred miles Dan could no longer go on, barely sat up straight, struggling to be awake and struggling to do anything, he drifted into a service station, thinking, 'We need to get some food, food and coffee that's all I need', rolling gently in to the service station the exhaustion was clear to see in his face, the last few days of stress and lack of sleep seemed to have aged him. As he stumbled off the bike Joanne grabbed at his arm, his look was quick and sharp, her smile melting his desire to demand to manage it alone.

The look in her face and the smile from her soul melted his hardened exterior, showing more of the real Dan each time she caught him like this, showing herself as an equal and demonstrating he could be loved as well as love. Strolling in to the service station, arm in arm she felt the love, no fear from what she has just done and no remorse. At times she was mentally harder than Dan and at times he was the stronger one, at this moment she led from the back, steering the ship, an equal partnership of two lost souls trying to create their own world, their way, for themselves. As they walked in the door together the air was thick with the smell of pastries, a woman serving fresh drinks and food, bright colours decorated the different types and the feeling of content washed over them.

The memory of Dan walking in on her doing exactly this warmed her entire body, creating a glow as she squeezes his arm; his sideways glance caught her with the biggest smile;

"What can I get you? I will never forget your face when I took your order I knew then you were special, Mr whatever else I can get."

The memory crept in to his mind stirring up that feeling sitting there smiling fantasizing about her, never would he have imagined the events that have now unfolded, in his typical style his thoughts, 'What next? Where next? How do I protect her? Does she need protecting? How the fuck are we going to fix this?' The confusion and worry battled against his happy thoughts, tearing them away from him, harming his mental state further and causing him yet more pain.

Sitting eating the pastries together she was satisfied, not thinking about what had happened or what will happen, not living in the past, not living in the future, just enjoying her coffee and the smells that wafted from the kitchen. Dan was a different beast frantically trying to take control of his situation, his mind and his life;

"We must move on this food is shit anyway, where is the greasy full English and a beautiful English Rose taking my order"

Joanne's smile was larger than ever, her eyes wide with delight, the more she knew Dan the more she 'got him', the more she knew what he meant and the stronger the connection grew the more equal they became, partners who could take on the world or escape it!

With food in his belly and coffee running through his veins the old Dan was back, the strong Dan, the man who wouldn't stop at anything to achieve his goals, ripping in to the miles and escaping the motorways, the pretty little villages now came and went, the roads small and tight with small animals roaming free in the street, as they rode through pretty hamlets with old cottages and chickens running free, people waved at him and nodded creating a state of confusion, 'are they just nice people or do they?' Tears flooded his eyes and a ball of sandpaper appeared in his throat, tearing at his strength, eroding it thought by thought, 'I am wearing the clothes and helmet from Morris and riding his bike, did they know him? Would they mourn his death? Should I stop and, no press on, I need to get to whatever Morris had in store for me. The 'Sat Nav' now showed 16 miles and 40 mins, they were getting ever closer to Morris's destination; the delight starts to come in waves, the hope of whatever Morris had created being exactly what they needed

Every mile felt more remote than the last and each mile climbed higher than before, the 'sat nav' counting down to the destination, with a feeling of nervousness wave after wave of anxiety, what would they find? Will it be safe? Could they stay forever? Would there be lots of people or some kind of solitude? Who is the person he owed a favour and why? The bushes thickened and became more unkempt, the ruggedness of the landscape creating a wild feeling, a feeling of remoteness a distance from civilisation.

Rounding the corner something was in the road, a large dead animal, it's blood running along the rough gravel surface, there was not enough room to pass with the chair attached. A small deer lay in front of them, as Dan started to drag it to one side, the deer's neck opened up, Dan recognised it was no cut but a vicious bite mark, fear ravaged his mind to what could have done this, hurriedly he got back to the bike to see a wolf with one ear and his hackles up looming into view with its teeth on full view, still with blood in its fur, its head low and its back arched.

Standing rooted to the spot fear running down his back petrifying him, the strong man reduced to a childlike motionlessness worsened by the growl of a lone wolf, as Dan mustered all his strength he turned for the bike and wolf leapt forward, teeth in view and the claws coming towards him, as the claws sunk into Dan's chest he turned his head away, grabbing it's legs, as he twisted to the ground the wolf bit at him and its teeth ripped deep into his arm, the pain excruciating, the blood feeling cold as it ran down inside his jacket. Wrestling with the wolf, pushing its head away the jaw of the wolf biting harder, splintering the bone in his arm, locking into a rolling mayhem of pain as they tumbled from side to side.

Each roll created more pain as claws and teeth stabbed away at Dan. Joanne was rising up from her chair with the new attitude she has developed, pointing the gun at the writhing bloody mess of man and beast, no clear way to shoot, no way to save her man, no way to take control of the situation. She fired the gun once into the air startling them both, as the wolf released its grip on his arm Dan kicked the wolf backwards, throwing it high into the air. Landing onto its side it yelped and jumped back on to its feet, this battle was not done and the wolf had a lesson to give and this lesson was not finished, it growled once more and bared it teeth.

Standing tall raising his head, grimacing through the pain Dan lifted both arms and roared like a bear at the wolf, the noise echoing around them all, the wolf did not move, it snarled and bared its teeth, they glistened in the light as the drool dripped from its mouth, it had the smell of his blood in his nostrils and the taste of it on his tongue.

In her now all too familiar way Joanne was stood with one foot on the seat and the other one raised onto the back, aiming the gun and looking straight down the barrel, the sight of the blood stained face of the wolf staring back at her, the grimace of a woman about to kill again slowly entering her mind and passing across her face, as she slowly starts to squeeze the trigger the wolf turned and ran leaving them both in a dazed confusion.

Rushing over to Dan she had not even took her finger off the trigger, throwing her arms around him, sending pain shooting up his arm from the bite, blood filling his glove and the pain filling his head, pushing her away he got on the bike, no words just survival as he kicked the engine of the bike over the pain engulfed his entire body, Barely able to keep his vision, he kicked it twice and the bike was alive again.

Every movement he made distressed him, every second was a lifetime as the pain became unbearable, his sight starting to blur and his mind silenced, his teeth forced together so hard he cracked one of his own teeth, the splintered tooth was now digging into his gum. His face was again contorted, angry and stony with the face of determination glaring out overpowering his mental and physical pain. Safety for Joanne was all that mattered and his only focus kept the pain secondary, the beast within him leading them forward, without thoughts, just instinct.

CHAPTER 14:

NEW BEGINNINGS

As Dan rolled in to a quaint little road with a few log cabins dotted along it he was barely conscious, consumed by the pain and tiredness which ravaged him, beating him down as he battled to keep his eyes open, the blurred view in front of him coming and going from his vison in and out like an old TV struggling for signal.

The 'sat nav' finally flashed; '*You have reached your destination.*' and he stalled the engine with a violet jerk throwing him against the tank of the bike, the lurch shocking Joanne from her sleepy state jolting her forwards too.

As she looked at her man peeling himself from the bike, using every ounce of his strength to even stand up, her horror as she saw him exhausted, swaying before her, the man she adored nearly beaten by this journey, nearly broken and looking literally half dead, still dripping blood from his arm on to the gravel road, as he stood trembling, close to death himself. The silence was suddenly shattered by an old man running down the road shouting;

"Morris, Morris, Morris"

Hearing that name collapsed his mind and brought him to tears which finally closed Dan's eyes as he dropped to the ground crying and wailing in more emotional pain than his arm could ever give him.

The old man crashed to the floor cradling him;

"Is this Dan? Where is Morris?

Joanne shook her head as her own tears formed;

"Morris saved us and sent us here to you, he said he owed you a favour for saving him; but he is now dancing his final waltz with Dotty in the sky"

The old man bowed his head, biting his lip and repressing the emotion that was clearly burning inside him;

"Morris was a good man, he owes me no favours, I owe him more than I could ever repay, but at the moment Dan needs help"

Dragging him to his feet, helping him walk towards the house, he stumbled every step, as he is led along the gravel path, delirious and repeating 'dad daaaddd daaaadddd' in a distressed voice, the quivering voice of a man who had hit rock bottom, a man with nowhere left to go, sitting at the bottom of a deep depression, no care or desires, his hopes muted and burned, a mind that is literally destroying itself, a mind that gently cries.

The log cabin was beautiful inside, old and retro with a few modern touches dotted about, clearly a house lived in, even a teapot and an open pack of biscuits are still on the table next to a wing back arm chair with an old record still spinning on the record player, a slight smell of a musty house, one not cleaned to the highest standard. As they lay Dan on to the sofa he whimpered like a child, regressing into a boy, pulling his knees up into his chest, they took a neatly folded blanket from the back of the sofa and lay it across him.

As he gently wept, his pain bleeding his soul as much as his blood oozed from his arm he opened his eyes to see the crochet blanket, he knew that blanket, Dotty had made that for him when he was poorly some 40 years ago;

"We need to call a doctor, we need an ambulance! How far to the hospital?"

The old man pulled out an old two way radio from his pocket shaking his head;

"We have no hospital and little supplies."

The radio crackles as he presses the mike button;

"Sofia, Sofia. It's Hans I need you at Morris's house, Dan is here he is bad, bring the medical box you copy?"

The crackling radio lets out a high-pitched distorted noise mixed in with a barely audible response;

"Copy I am on the way is Morris there?"

As Hans turned his head towards Joanne barely making eye contact, he stuttered and stifled his own feelings his wrinkled nose and stern lips giving him away, the hurt and upset causing him great pain;

"We all owe Morris especially my wife; don't tell her about Morris, please save that for later"

Joanne nodded in confusion as she knelt down next to the sofa, gently resting her head against Dan, as she felt his laboured breaths, each one torturing her with worry.

As Sofia rushed in with the medical supplies, her shock was evident her eyes wide and her mouth open, Hans took Joanne gently by the arm;

"Leave this to my wife I think I need to tell you a little story."

As he led her outside to a wonderfully kept garden with climbing roses and wandering wisteria plants dangling around a bench he gestured for her to sit;

"I am sorry I don't know your name, we are Sofia and Hans I cannot do enough for Morris and his wishes."

Her shaky voice quivered out her name as she dropped her head into her hands. Without even looking up she explained how Morris pulled them from the water and sent them here, but Morris shot himself on the dock dressed in Dan's clothes, he really did save us but left us too.

As Hans wiped away his own tears shaking his head;

"Morris saves everyone that what he does, the only person he could not save is himself"

Hans' tears were overflowing from his eyes as he explained the day Morris came into their lives. Morris had ridden into the little village at the base of the Harz Mountains, we had been at a market and were walking back when a small pack of wolves attacked us, Sofia tried to scare them off and took the majority of the injuries as I froze. His face clearly showed his regret, the wolves were tearing at her flesh and clawing at her, Morris drove that bike and side car straight at the pack of wolves running them over and scattering the rest across the road killing them instantly, but the one wolf was still biting and clawing at my wife and I could do nothing as she lay motionless bleeding whilst the wolf continued to maul her, Morris stood in the side car and shot that wolf, taking its ear clean off, as the wolf fled Morris brought us home in his sidecar and nursed her back to health, he had done some time as a medic in the military he said. We owe him our life so much so we named our son Otto as he was always telling me about the Otto cycle of an engine when he tried to teach me how his bike engine worked.

Joanne's face motionless and pale like she had seen a ghost;

"That wolf that attacked us had one ear! It attacked the memory of Morris not Dan, it thought he was Morris"

The look from Hans was subtle but all knowing, considering his thoughts as a wise man would;

"Joanne. Wolves are a strange breed and as much as we know about them we know so little, the wolf is a master good or bad, he is a teacher and for some reason you needed to learn, maybe you needed to realise how hard life can be, maybe you needed to know how to endure hardship before true happiness or maybe when to stop roaming"

Her mind was revolving faster than a spinning top, faster than she could keep up with;

"Do you think we are safe now?"

Slowly Hans sat back in to his chair;

"No one is ever safe my dear, nobody has every truly made it, it's just a battle to stay the right side up! This house was my dad's house, he built the 3 houses here and he gave them all to me when he died. We are completely off grid, no connection to the outside world, solar and wind power is all we have and no internet, Sofia is a nurse and will bring Dan back to health and as I said we have a debt to Morris, as he is no longer here we owe that debt to you two now"

A gentle soft German voice dances across the garden tiptoeing into their ears;

"Joanne, he is calling for you."

She kissed Hans on the forehead and rushes into the house to see the recovery of all recoveries. Dan sat with his bandaged arm and his bandaged chest, bright eyed, sipping from a tea cup with his one good hand;

"Not my usual brew this honey and turmeric water but it's like rocket fuel I tell ya"

As Hans and Sofia stood in the doorway, they smiled and nodded to each other, no words but communication shouting loud and clear, as Joanne 'hugged the life out of Dan' who was still trying to sip on his new brew;

"I will be back to change those bandages in a few hours but get some rest, and tonight we will bring dinner over I feel we need to get to know each other"

As the two slumped into the large wing-backed sofa together they melted into each other as one, being joined by the marriage of two equal minds sharing the same space, as they drifted in to a hazed sleep their completeness grows and neither of had ever felt so secure and relaxed, as they do now, in complete isolation from the troubles of the world, no place to be no place to go, not living in the past or the future just the beautiful moment they share as they lay for hours drifting in and out of sleep.

Sofia and Hans stood once again in the doorway but this time with Otto, the trio of happiness as one. Sofia and Hans were well into retirement age and Otto mid-teens, no flashy fashions just simple functional clothes and muddy walking boots.

"Otto go put these on the table with your dad we will be through shortly"

As Sofia woke them up gently they stirred from a place they had never been;

"Joanne if you could help Hans and Otto in the kitchen I will tend to these wounds"

As she unwrapped the bandages Dan returned to the hard man he is, hiding his pain conveying a stern, stony and stubborn look;

"You remind me of Morris, a tough man but with a kind heart he once did this for me and maybe it was even the same wolf who taught us both that we need to rest not move on like a rolling stone"

No words were returned but he felt she understood the question in his mind and she answered it before he could ask it;

"Yes I was wayward, I was a vagabond, a rolling stone lost in the world, I had the desire to move along constantly and move away from this calmness, the wolf taught me I need both, I learned I needed to rest and be away from the world but visit it on my terms when I need it, Morris taught me the rest and I showed him a way to escape his troubles a way to silence the questions in his mind with answers, I am going to treat these wounds with a raw honey and turmeric paste plus a few little secrets that I blend to stop the infection, the honey and turmeric water you were drinking will help too for many reasons."

The meal on the large table was huge with a vast array of colours and foods, everything fresh and everything with more taste than they could have ever imagined, bread still warm and softer than a babies pillow, with the food exciting their senses and delighting every fibre of them, the most cutting question of all came from Otto;

"What happened to Morris? Nobody is talking about him, we are eating in his house but he is not here."

The looks around the table speak volumes and Otto nodded;

"He died saving you didn't he?"

As the young man swallowed the news hard and his eyes opened wide;

"He told me if I saw you here without him to tell you, he did it for you and all this is yours, my time has been and gone, now shine."

Dan placed the cutlery down and put one hand on the back of his own neck, feeling ill once again, the intake of breath Dan made felt like it sliced his chest wide open but he did not weep or crumble he simply said;

"Morris created my escape and my life, he saved me when I was a boy and now he has saved my life as a man, he died in honour of his love"

The room glowed it felt like it answered back like Morris was there agreeing with him no voices just agreements.

The silence was interrupted by Hans;

"This is and always will be the house we gave to Morris, in his absence it's now yours, travel on my road for a while till you find yours again"

Joanne looked straight in to Dan's eyes and smiled, he knew she wanted to stay;

"My road is the same as Morris, my true dad so I think I have found my road and it ends here if you will have me?"

The moment hung, lasting for eternity, the contended feelings overwhelming as the room and answers clearly without words;

"Morris scoured the country buying his delights, he earned well from renovating old machinery and making stuff that hadn't worked in years' work again, a real handy man who could turn his hand to anything. As you travel through the villages anything that runs, ticks or moves Morris has worked on at some point, he was always happy with a few tools in his sidecar and a machine to go and fix in the villages, although he rarely slept, sometimes I would hear him in the place he worshiped the most, Otto take them through the room Morris loved the most"

As they step though a doorway a vast room opened up, a room with every part of a 50's biker café laid out in front of them, a juke box in one corner and a counter in the other, tables chairs and memorabilia, engine casings hung on the wall and parts of engines polished and mounted on wooden plaques. Otto looked in to their faces and spoke with a huge grin;

"That's not all"

He held out his hand and pointed behind them. As the two turned, Dan is stunned, a car park inside the café full of various bikes all parked next to the café tables.

"Morris always said in his moment of weakness these bikes lift him up and all he needed to finish it off was his beautiful wife to share a brew with while they sat in the café. I guess you two finish his dream off, a dream he could never turn into reality without Dotty"

As Otto left he pressed a button on the juke box and the 50's music poured out;

"So what can I get you Mr whatever else I can get?"

Dan managed a half smile through his twisted grief, a smile so obviously trying to suppress his tormented mind. He wandered over to the counter and flicked the coffee machine on, it burst into life, as it prepared to warm his soul with his brew of choice he looked back to see the vast array of bikes, mostly chrome collectables, a workshop come museum come café it was the perfect shed built fantasy, made perfect by his leather clad biker chick stood amongst them all, his love and his destiny, in fact his whole life stood before him, surrounded by all the bikes he could ever dream of, as the coffee cup finished its fill, he felt complete, placing it on the counter for Joanne and starting another brew in the machine, a real smile burst through;

"Welcome home honey we made it."

His head turned slowly as he said the words and he winked at her with a small smile rippling across his face. As he swept her into his arms he drew her in close, swinging her to the side like a 50's rock roll dance, she melted, feeling the moment as her own and special only to them. As she strutted over to the bikes;

"They all have keys in do they run?"

"I am sure they do and if Morris has worked on them, but there will be surprises on each one like that fuel tank under the side car, as we sat at the side of the road with no money and barely any fuel, I was lost mentally and thought there is no way I can save us both and Morris had already saved us with that invention."

As Dan took a deep breath and his face sunk as low as his heart, she wandered back into his arms pulling him in tight;

"You're right Morris saved us, he saved us when we needed fuel and money and when he joined Dotty on that dock, in his final dance with her he gave us our escape, but without you I could not have escaped, without you I would still be working 12 hour shifts and serving all day breakfasts to middle aged overweight truckers, without you I am nothing, you saved me like Morris saved us"

As the barrage of thoughts attacked his mind, question after question literally stabbing his mind evoking a pain like no other;

"But why did he kill himself, why couldn't he share this with us? Rather than leaving us?"

As Joanne placed both her hands onto his tear soaked beard, as always she could smell the coffee on his breath and see the pain inside him, she raised a half smile and tiltined her head to one side, she forced his head upwards so his tear filled eyes met hers;

"He built this for you, but without Dotty to share his life with, his heart was quiet and his mind slow, all the wonders of this very place dull, when you love someone everything is at full volume, for Morris his world was on mute, the day she died his life ended, but he stuck around long enough to right the wrong in his head for you, a home away from the herds of the world, a home with all the things that remind you of him and Dotty, but they also reminded him of Dotty, once he had saved you, his work was done and it was time for him to be with Dotty again"

Dan shook his head, slowly tossing words and answers to her point around in his head, wanting to argue wanting to prove her wrong, but in his heart he knew she was right;

"You do realise we need to honour them Joanne, we need to make them proud."

Joanne looks him straight in the eye and with a smile as bright as the sunshine on summer day;

"You already do, you are a good man, with morals and respect, that is all they would have wanted from you."

Slowly nodding and agreeing with her, guided by her wise words which wander through his mind, he leads her over to a red leather American style 50's diner bench seat;

"He always said he wanted one of these in his shed at home and I thought he was crazy, this is my paradise I love it."

The pair lay arm in arm across the seat floating off into a dream, a dream of a life far enough from society they could avoid it but close enough so they could dip their toe in when they wanted to.

They had no internet, no phones and nothing with any modern communication in it, power was created on site with solar and wind power. They had escaped the old life they led and made it to the perfect off the grid hideout, one where they could live out their days in seclusion, with the memories from the ride of their life, tearing up the world before they escaped it.

As the morning sun poked itself through the skylight Joanne opened her eyes to see Dan working on a bike already, just tinkering with a few tools adjusting something on a bike his hands dirty and his mind contented, his smile to himself real and the pleasure of the bikes so evident, they may have escaped the world but this was Dan's escape from his mind;

"Morning darling are you okay why didn't you wake me? Do you think you can be happy here; will your rolling stone now grow some moss?

His laugh warmed her entire being as his found himself displaying the happiness he always should have had, content in his own space, but the troubles are only repressed and his 'Pandora's box', already bursting with pain and bad memories, tucked away in the back of his mind, wrapped up and hidden from view but smoldering away like a firework about to ignite.

As Joanne left him tinkering in the garage, she enjoyed the thought of happy Dan in her mind she almost skipped her way into her paradise, the smell of the coffee pot brewing brought back memories of her old life, fond memories she didn't realise she had of her old life. The memories pleased her but more because it's wasn't her future now, the last few weeks had taught her a lot about her inner self and the desire to experience life at high volume then relax and enjoy the feeling. As she put the tin of coffee back in the cupboard she notices an old coffee tin with three letters on it DMT.

The letters running through her head, what could they mean? Not really knowing Morris but realising he was a deep-thinking man, maybe even deeper than Dan in the way he must have thought, this must be important it's next to the coffee. As she carefully lifted the tin out, it's lid bent and battered, the label worn and old, clearly heavily used, as she prized the lid off, one of her favorites smells only sweeter wafted up in to her nostrils, the sweet smell of new shoes intoxicating her from small yellow and white flowers.

In a moment of complete confusion her thoughts danced around her mind, '*What is this? Why does it smell so sweet?*'

"*Dan! Dan, come here look at this!*"

As he begrudgingly left his play pen of metal desire, feeling like the call from a long marriage, the call of something that surely couldn't be important enough to need him to stop playing with this old classic chrome beauty.

Trying not to sound annoyed;

"*What is it?*"

Showing him the tin she raised her eyebrows telling him she had as much idea as he did as to what this is;

"*I guess it's some herbal blend of something Morris had been playing with.*"

Being the kind of curious motivated man that Dan was, he grabbed the two way radio and the coffee tin;

"*Sofia, Hans do you copy, do u read me? What is DMT? Over.*"

His voice urgent and forceful, Dan rarely meant to sound like a sergeant major but his natural voice often came across as arrogant and forceful, The few silent seconds slipped by like infuriating hours for Dan, pressing the button again trying desperately not to sound harsh or impatient;

"Do you copy? Is DMT some kind of hippy happy herbal tea or should I smoke it?   Over."

The silence once again frustrated Dan's impatience. As he tossed the radio on the side a response crackled through the old speaker;

"I copy, don't touch it I am on my way over I thought Morris had stopped using   that."

The two of them staring at the coffee tin with more questions than actually comprehendible, which raucously rampage round in their minds. What would it be? Sofia had sounded so harsh, in a way they had not heard, almost sounding as if she was a headmistress of an old public school, as she slowly walked in the door her face was emotionless, not the lady they had shared dinner with and not the nurse who tended to his wounds, not the face of a caring woman.

"Hans does not agree with it, he thinks it can do as much bad as good, I myself thinking it's the secret to understanding, enlightenment and true happiness, however sometimes like that wolf bite it needs to do harm before it can do good."

Dan's stern face and confidence, with his raised bearded chin glaring across the room;

"If Morris used it then, that's good enough for me!"

Shaking her head and looking at the pair of them pensive and unsure of the reaction;

"I am not sure either of you are ready for it but I am not sure anybody is ever ready for Ayahuasca or as Morris preferred to call it DMT he always preferred technical terms."

As she explained in depth it's a drink traditionally to absorb the dimethyltryptamine, if you want to revelate your soul, find your inner demons and really know how to beat them this is the way, but if you're not strong enough for the message it will destroy your view of yourself and the world, it's a lesson and with that you need to grow with what you learn, some describe meeting mother nature who will answer all the questions you have, some describe meeting the Devil himself and often as Morris found lost loved ones.

Dan's face came alive with excitement;

"Fuck yeah lets brew it up I have more questions than I can handle, I fancy a conversation with someone to ask what the fuck my life is about?"

Sofia's face showing her worry and frustrating Dan;

"All the ingredients are here but it will take a few hours to make it up properly you may want to get cleaned up, this could be messy enough anyway"

As Sofia started to gently boil some water and carefully mix in the ingredients to multiple pots;

"Don't forget to clean your mind too, clear away all the negativity and relax."

The two could not be in more contrast, Dan full of excitement and Joanne full of fear;

"Are you going to do this Dan?"

He did not speak but his silence was more words than she needed, of course he was going to do it, when had Dan ever not chosen the crazy option? Dan stripped down to his underwear, closed his eyes and shook his hands by his waist, loosening up like he was warming up for a boxing match, light on his toes as he literally bounced up and down.

The room was silent and Dan sat on the floor his mind cleared, well as clear as Dan could make it, Joanne anxiously fiddling with her poker straight dark hair, Slowly and gently Sofia brought in a single glass on a silver tray, with a reddish brown substance clinging to the glass like milk does;

"Aya-Waska for one my friend, enjoy and may the spirits answer all your questions"

Laying the silver tray down in front of Dan, Sofia started to chant and seemed to be calling the spirits as Dan took the glass and gulped it down in one go, the vile thick liquid dragging its way down his throat, struggling to keep the vile brew down, his face twisted in a battle between vomit and answers. Taming the beast and keeping the drink down was only the start of it as the sickness hit him harder than a boxer, knocking him on to his back and cramping his stomach, grasping at the sofa and gasping for air, he looked like he was once again dying.

Sofia gestured at Joanne to stay out the way with a single finger raised in the air telling her to stay like a dog, Joanne was stunned by the quick harshness Sofia had showed her, but this only added to her fears which grows larger with every passing second, Joanne's fears grew and plagued her, wanting to stop him, to end this temporary suffering, but the wheels were now in motion as Sofia sat with Dan chanting and holding his hands as he became lifeless and still;

"He has begun his journey all we can do now is wait."

CHAPTER 15:

ROAMING NO MORE

Dan was rolling and bucking on the floor clutching his stomach, saliva dribbling from his mouth, his back hunched over and his eyes tightly shut with tears streaming down his face. Sofia hadn't even moved a muscle, her eyes focused showing the seriousness of her thoughts, but every fiber of Joanne ached in pain as she watched Dan tortured again. As he flopped back onto the floor with the suggestion of a heroin type high, euphoria written across his face, Sofia raised her head and started to chant, slowly raising her hands, making no sense to Joanne as the rhythm of the words flowed and danced around the room. Dan lay on the floor slowly twitching and foaming at the mouth with his body rigid, developing a fear in Joanne more than she'd ever had before.

As the seconds turned to minutes and the minutes turned to several, it felt like hours had passed as Dan lay motionless on the floor. His dried saliva collected in his beard and his teeth tightly clenched together, the room was shrouded, subdued and silent, fear of the unknown and fear of the known attacking Joanne as she knew so much of Dan's dark past and feared he may be re-living it, suspended in solitude battling with his own mind.

Sofia floated around the room waving around some sage, wafting the soft smoke around the room, still chanting under her breath as Dan started to moan and groan, rolling on to his side they rushed to him and supported him, the loudest battle cry screamed out from the twisted face of a man fighting, his eyes wide open and his mouth fully open, screaming as if galloping into battle, throwing his arms around. A silver back gorilla had emerged, the pair dodged the crushing blows which thrust towards them as he leapt to his unsteady feet, staggering around shouting his battle cry in a torrent of abuse;

"Mother fuckers will never take me down, never I tell ya never!!!!"

The words turn to deranged rambling as Dan fought with imaginary somethings, lunging, ducking and dodging, wrestling with whatever occupied the world in his head, the aggression bouncing around the room from Dan scaring Joanne, the fear crushing her hope, Dan is poles apart from this, smashing anything his fists come into contact with, wildly kicking and often protecting his face with his large forearms, a switch had flicked and everything in the room is being destroyed with a roar, a lion warning to whoever he can see he looks akin to every exorcism Joanne has seen in the movies, uncontrolled violet and enraged with evil.

They stood with their backs against the wall hoping and praying they would not be in the path of destruction as the unstable, bearded, wild man tore around the room, knocking over tables throwing the wingback chair at the wall. The war cries slowly simmered to silence and the rage started to calm, Dan staggered over to the wing back chair lay on its back, standing it upright with one hand, he slumped into it and his eyes flickered till he rested easy in the chair, wilting in the old chair from the wild man to the sleeping man;

"Joanne let's leave him to it he will sleep for a few hours now, everybody does."

They sat in the garden sipping on the same herbal brew Sofia had made for Dan, the air now calm but the worry still high. Over the last few hours Joanne had heard about the time that Morris had used the DMT and answered many of his questions but also met many of his inner demons, his main demons had been not being there to protect his wife when she was murdered and not being able to face going back to look after Dan;

"He so wanted to come back and many times he tried but before the day ended, I always heard his bike roll by the house and back into the garage, he fitted that extra tank to the sidecar too come back and try and talk Dan into coming to live here, but every time he tried he cried so much over his dead wife he never made into France let alone England, he must really have meant it this time, but I guess that's why he danced his way across the water to meet his wife".

The thought of the love that he had for his wife always warmed Joanne, but this time she was still cold, fearing the worst for Dan and worried for who or what he was fighting within that rage. The garden was peaceful and tranquil and the thought of maintaining it to this standard was not something Joanne thought she would be able to do. The clumping of heavy boots shuffling across the cobbled path delighted Joanne as she leapt to her feet, showering Dan with affection. Affection he was not ready for, he draped his arms around her but no feelings returned, no love just hollowness;

"Dan what happened? Are you okay?"

Dan grumbled and mumbled some half words as Sofia passed him a steaming hot coffee. The delight lit Dan's eyes as he sipped at his brew, slurping away till the warmth returned to his body;

"Everybody was there, everybody, literally everybody, Morris, Dotty, my parents and everyone I have ever crossed, even that poor boy lay hanging out of his car, everybody who has been significant in my life was there, but most of all an unknown, a giver and a receiver, questions and answers. She was like calm in a storm, as the pandemonium and millions of voices shouted over each other to talk to me, she was quiet yet loud, always there always heard, so much to process I think I need to be walk alone for a while!"

Sofia led Joanne away gently reassuring her and stroking her arm as they walked along the cobbled path;

"Dan there is a full pot of coffee there and a pot of my herbal brew, drink whichever helps you the most but take all the time you need, this garden is the best place to be to collect your thoughts"

He sat with his chin on his chest and once again the weight of his world on his shoulders but this time clarity, new ideas and new thoughts, Dan was dead but Dan was alive and reborn, a new version of himself.

As the light faded and the hours passed, the solar lights started to flicker into life, Joanne calmly walked down the path with flowers in her hair and a flowing dress. Dan was stunned, her inner beauty overpowering her physical beauty, the yellow coloured flowers were really 'popping' against her black hair. Radiating her content feelings and sitting beside the wild man, she saw something new in him, she saw a sparkle in his eye he had never had before, a genuine full face smile erupted across his face as he hugged her and whispered the three magic words he had always wanted to truly mean;

"I love you."

Her heart burst open with happiness. She could see the love and feel it, Dan was different yet the same, old yet new and more importantly he looked happy;

"Dan what happened?"

As his new warm look engulfed her, his smile radiating more love than she could comprehend;

"I see a little different, many people stood before me and humbled me, there is so much more to this life, yet we actually need less than we think we do"

As Dan explained with the excitement of a child the experience he had just had, he even spoke nicely of his dad;

"He did not cope, he had done wrong and he deserves to be hated but he was a weak man. I have learned from him, I am a better man because I learned from him. I learned what not to be in life. An elderly woman I still do not know explained to me that if we gained from the experience it was not a bad experience long term and bad experiences are only temporary".

The delight in Dan was so obvious, his shoulders were higher, his face brighter, his eyes alive. He was new and he was stronger, answering questions Joanne didn't even know were in his head. His speech went on but every word was life-affirming for him and anybody he could tell. He was like a wise old master fully in control of his thoughts and clear on his direction. But now the thought-provoking questions were deeper;

"What do you see of yourself? Can you even look yourself in the eye? What do you see really deep down? When you dig deep enough into your personality, what would you change? Would you like you self it you were to meet yourself?"

This was the question that hit Joanne the hardest.

"We are all free, but we choose to be enslaved, we choose not to break free, the question begs; am I free or am I trapped? Who would know? We all know really we are trapped, freedom is nothing else left to loose. Satisfaction is better than money or possessions....why? Because success is measured by others and satisfaction is measured by yourself! I was warned at the start by the old lady, she told me. No one can judge your life but you, as nobody can ever fully understand it but you, if you judge yourself and have regret, the darkness unfolds and you need to make steps to repair it. The worst thing in life is to wait to your death bed to revelate your life, everyone revelates, but do they change before they regret the mistakes that could have been fixed? Are you happy? Did you do the things that made you smile? Did you actively set the wheels in motion or wait for it to happen? If so did it ever happen or just fade away into an old disused dream? Did you take that trip? Did you stretch your mind? Did you challenge your very being past its boundaries or did you sit in a hazy bubble content wasting life, waiting for it to happen whilst you sit in front of the TV allowing the seconds, hours, years and decades to slip towards old age, ! The average age is 80 years old, that's less than 30,000 days and a little over 700,000 hours, life is short many people spend 40 hours at work a week and the working life is about 50 years, if you take this out plus the time you sleep there is not much life left! Worse if you waste it procrastinating, never doing just waiting, sitting and complaining, you could actually waste the few days you have to live, never realising it till your old and frail, no longer able to use your days well, how many days do you exist? Not actually living! How many days do you actually live!"

The advice Dan enjoyed the most in his chemical revelation was, 'If you're not happy with you lives make a change or make several but make them change, go forward and make it a positive journey! The secret to change, is to focus on the new not the old, doing everything to make it change, things can only change if you set the wheels in motion and keep turning them.' This was actually Dan's life being explained to him, telling him he had done well, he had made the changes, but along the way made mistakes, however the mistakes were learned from, questions and revelations made him grow to someone better at every opportunity of his life. The bad becomes good if you grow from it, rather than let it consume you.

As Dan sat in his happy hazy headspace, he muttered;

"We have made it to our utopia, we are free to live how we want free from constraints, I used too ask what did I want? Now I know, what I want is to live my life doing the things that please us, not society, not our friends, most don't understand our desire or our life, but we have succeeded in freeing ourselves from the daily 'hamster wheel of life' we are in charge of our happiness, leading ourselves forward. But Joanne what do you want, what is your dream? I had forgotten to check you were getting what you want. I forgot to create our life I was just living mine as one not as us."

Her face was thoughtful and confused, she was worn out by the enthusiasm he was showing, the energy he had and the speed at which his mind was moving forward and developing his thoughts;

"What I want is animals, I was to raise as many animals as possible, rescue sick ones too and nurse them back to health, just like Morris clearly did with his machines. The pair of us have our loves, our desires and come together to help, we each can have our goals and our satisfaction of achieving our desires as we sit on this bench watching the sun go down, we can share our hopes, dreams and successes, that satisfy our souls"

The contented feeling flooded through him, the warmth it created allowed him to share his darker experiences with no regret or sorrow, for he had gained from them;

"There were some darker times as I stood with our maker, she told me about my rage and the destruction I had caused, they were noble but wrong, I thought I was going crazy but I needed to learn, I needed to protect. It's no different to nature and animals, especially pack animals. We need to have destruction but keep it to necessity, not sport, not greed not for power but to keep the status quo. She answered my life long questions about me and many other humans who do not play nicely together"

Joanne's face showed how troubled and worried she was about this revelation, what was he going to say, who is he, what makes him tick? Had she missed something?

"We are the lone packers we need our groups but we need our space, too much of one or the other puts us out of balance, I need to be part of my pack but spend time lone wolf too, allowing me to recharge. Those that don't spend enough time alone become confused, agitated and led by the desires of others, not following their true destiny as the pack clouds the yearning, the desires become that of the pack not the individual, without time to reflect on our own we are lost, lost in a group, the irony when we are with a group we are lost, when we are alone we are found! But we must do both regularly or we are lost not following our true direction. We are the 'loan packers' I thought we were, a species that needs both a pack and solitude!"

The thought of this had troubled Dan for many years trying to work out which he should be doing when actually it should have been both. He was running from himself, running from his life, running from his own fears rather than facing them and growing from them;

"Is your life complete then Dan?"

The words caused him to laugh and to shake his head as if he had heard the most foolish thing ever;

"No never there is so much more to become, so much more to be, so much living to be had, but I have found my peace, even over the deaths and destruction that plague my life, I did wrong and discussed it with each and every one of them whilst I floated around with the old lady, they forgave me as they had done wrong and I had done wrong, we both had done wrong and we both had learned, we both carried the pain of our crimes and are better people because of it, nobody dies, consciousness lives on and continues as we remain here in this mortal space, they take it with them and become enlightened by the actions in this life, this life is just a stepping stone to something far bigger than I could see but it was there I had a glimpse"

The only thing Dan feared is what remained undone, what was unfinished, what had not been fixed, his biggest fear that could not be answered was Indy, what would become of her? What would happen to her? Had he damaged a rare delicate flower and turned her to stone? Had he killed her spirt? She did not cope with the anger, the death, destruction or a power struggle; she would have liked it here, but was it too late to save her from the rippling effect set in motion when she killed that guy in the petrol station to save me? Will she ever recover from it? As that had not yet played out, no answers could be gained only hope!

One thing Dan had gained from his dance with the old lady was everything can be changed and everything is a lesson good or bad, if you gain a better understanding of life you win in the end, nobody truly loses unless they do nothing and drift through life till the end, or worse chase false idols of success thinking they are successful, when really they have missed out, distracted by money, careers and possessions. As you face your maker with all the money and success, are you satisfied? Did you love? Or did you shroud it with wealth and fake love? All the money, power and success mean very little as you lie on your death bed revelating your life! You can get someone to make you money, drive your car, but you cannot pay for someone to die for you! Once life has slipped by you cannot buy more, don't forget to make time for your life, for you and your loved ones, as when you face the final steps, you will regret, you will not be satisfied, you will have missed out on true happiness, when the clock strikes for your death, whether you are in a small house or a mansion if you have missed out on life, you still missed out, if you die in a limousine or an old wreck of a car, you still die the same, the material things are distractions to your true life and satisfaction, hiding it under a false veil of happiness. Educated to be rich is not the same as educated to be satisfied, the difference between being human and a human being is your choices, only a few really ever really get this.

Joanne and Dan had finally found their world, they understood what they wanted from life and how to live it, the past lay outside that world and past couldn't find them, cut off protected and hidden in a dreamland of happiness, a life built on the desire and the likes of two individuals who came together as one.

As the years rolled by so did the joy of their secluded life, frequent trips to most of Europe on various motorbikes that Morris had built, the simplistic beauty of being inside a helmet incognito and hidden from the masses, retreating back to the hidden privacy away from society and away from the negativity of the modern world, smiles came easy and so did the feeling of content, recharging themselves ready for the next excursion back into the metropolitan beautiful cities and culture, with the all too familiar hum of the rushed and difficult lives the herds and sheeple blindly following their lives, bluring from selfie to selfie, not seeing the beauty they have around them, chasing false idols and trying to reach the pot of gold at the end of the rainbow, stepping on each other competing to be the best at nothing that truly matters.

The life they had created was a delight, calm and contented when they wanted and fast paced when they chose to roam the wonders of the surrounding towns and countries, seeing all the pleasures but having no stress, no job to rush back to and no hamster wheel to run in, a life they did not need a break from, for life rolled forward like the ever turning wheels of the bikes that hid them from society as they roamed free.

As the pair sat drinking their favorite brew on the pristine little part of the world they had sitting on a carved wooden bench with a little table in front of them, Dan looked over and winked;

"I think my rolling stone has grown a little moss, I don't think I will ever want to go back to the normal world, this is how I dreamed life would be, on our terms doing as we please"

The look in Joanne's eyes answered him loud and clear as her words radiated from her soul to his, there were one and they didn't need anybody else, the sun was just starting to peek above the trees and the smell of a new day engulfed their senses, illuminating their day. As each leaf moved on the trees in the breeze, the sun flickered through to them, hypnotising the pair into the hedonistic state they had both become so accustomed to, so much so it was a daily drug they needed, sitting in the perfection of their lives, untouchable and unshakeable.

Joanne was so nearly dosing off in the early morning sun and Dan was watching her, idolising her, with memories of when he first saw her strut across to tease him whilst taking his breakfast order. They had come so far in more ways than one, but something had 'pricked' at Dan and he felt uneasy, an odd feeling crept over him, familiar yet old, a feeling of worry a feeling of horror, as his ears tuned into the sound of a thumping V-twin and old one too, carburetor old and running rough too, as the noise grew so did his unrest, his eyes wide and his skin electrified as he questioned himself; 'Surely that's not a bike coming here, it sounds like Jack's bike how would he have found me? Why would he have found me? What the fuck is he doing here?' A feeling of his utopia starting to crumple flooded through his mind, fear climbs up his neck, seeping into his mind.

Dan stood tall with the sneer of a sergeant major; 'who the fuck could it be?' The serene beauty of his moment shattered by the recognisable noise of a bike that was not meant to be here, one glance at Joanne showed his concern. As he tried to conceal it, she leaned forward and tried to take his hand, but a Dan she has not seen for a while was back, an angry worried and scared Dan stood once again in front of her. As a silhouette of a single bike with a solo rider loomed into view, the noise grew and the silhouette unfolded, it is Jack and he is riding along in the usual slow and controlled way he had, cruising along the road to their little place of sanctuary but why and how?

As Jack leaned the bike on its side stand a moment of silence hung in the air as he turned the bike off, no excitement, no rush to find out why or how he has found them. The feeling inside Dan was sorrowful, thinking if someone had found him then anyone could find him and his whole world could come crashing down in an instant;

"Well fuck me you're a 'ard man to track down aren't you? Aren't you going to welcome me to your humble abode?"

As Dan's pensive look fell away allowing a small awkward smile to ripple across his face he slowly walked across to his old friend and wrapped his arms tightly around him, giving him the hug of a brother;

"I thought I was far enough off the grid I couldn't be found that all, just very surprised to see anyone ride up that road."

The old biker stepped back from him, the intensity building as he stared at Dan long and hard, his face was stern and aged, just like his black leather jacket, his grubby black jeans and his old scruffy boots spoke loudly for him just like his old V-twin he rode in on.

The stare burned though Dan, the 1000 yard stare of a man with something important on his mind, something biting at him and causing him pain. As Jack opened his mouth the gruff voice drummed its way into Dan's ears;

"We have a problem you see. When Indy left that night as you dropped into the water, a butterfly effect of that ride had started, she was no longer the delicate flower she was, she was different she had changed and I kept in touch even though she never replied to me, but now that butterfly effect has been eaten by a big fucking bird and we my friend are responsible, and to that end we owe her!"

He pulled out a handful of pictures as he thrust them at Dan, his grubby oil stained hands showed the mark of his life. Scars and oil were the words on his page, but the pictures told a different story, pictures of a high society posh woman. As Dan looked closer it was Indy;

"This is not the Indy I remember."

As he flicked though the pictures a bloated face, blood-stained and beaten turned the old Dan back on, the rage causing him to physically shake and his emotions to flood his eyes.

Joanne peered over his shoulder and gasped;

"What happened to her?"

Jack turned his head always and started to fiddle with his bike;

"It's long fuckin' story princess, but that night set a path for her and a very different life unfolded, now the prick with the money is seeking revenge on her for fucking him over as she left him, that was not the last picture she sent me after he took her back, the last one in that deck tells it how it is"

As Dan drew the last picture out, the image of her beaten face crying with a scrawled message scribbled across it; 'Please set me free, free like Dan!'

The message hit Dan in the face like a punch square on the nose; a sickness quickly engulfed him and the rage of emotions flooded back into him, he had fell into the same trap as Morris, enjoying himself so much he had forgotten the trouble he had left behind;

"Dan we can't go we can't leave here you are a wanted man!"

Joanne rushed her words nervous and squeaky, she knew what would happen next, he turned his nose up and scowled like she had forgotten he did, his words barked out with the aggression of a hungry wolf;

"I owe her, without her we never would have met Jack, never got out of England and never ended up here! Come with me or don't, but I leave and I leave now!"

Jack avoided looking at Joanne, turning his smile away, his thoughts happy that Dan was the man he always thought he was, a man of morals and strength a man willing to risk everything for honour, the Viking of man that people said he was all those years ago. Dan was already in the garage throwing stuff in a duffel bag, crudely strapping it to a bike Joanne had never actually been on, a bike that Dan rarely even started, a solid black paint job against a chromed frame, a perfectly polished triple exhaust barely long enough to reach past the riders foot peg. This was a bike of two halves, a shiny garage queen with off road tyres and a huge engine, straight wide bars and no fairing. A beast of a bike built to take on anything, a small badge riveted to the perfectly crafted frame; 'For Dan from Dad, forever with you through anything and everything'.

As Dan started the bike the triple twisted engine rocked it way into life, as he blipped the throttle flames shot out from the exhaust, a lump in his throat nearly choked him, never had he ridden this bike out of this road. Morris had built this with Dan's personality in mind, it fitted him like a glove and every detail was for Dan by Morris, every little modification was a reflection of Dan's personality, this bike was Dan.

Sat on the bike he was once again fighting with his own mind, the vibrations of the bike bringing him to life, as Joanne touched him lightly on the shoulder;

"If you go, we go as one. Just like always, we are stronger together than alone"

Roaring out of the café/garage with the juke box still playing but silenced with the sound of the triple monster echoing around it and the flames lighting up the room, the glee covered Jack's face as he witnessed the full glory of the bike charging towards him;

"That's one sweet motherfucking battleship brother!"

As Jack spun his bike around on the dirt road, spinning the rear wheel leaving his mark and throwing up his usual dust storm, the trio screamed off down the road with the sound of a deranged banshee, both engines straight pipes no baffles and raw, brutal brawn and bolshie like the riders, who bring with them revelations for the honour of their beloved friend Indy, leaving the dust to settle around the coffee cups left on the table, empty like the dreams they once held!

…To be continued in the "Search of The Revelator"

About the Author

Mark Huck was born in 1970s, growing up in the fast paced 1980s living an adrenaline filled life, with sports and fast cars; as his life became more complex he found his solidarity in the simplicity of the open road and the world of motorbikes.

After leaving school with barely any qualifications, his love of engines led him to become a vehicle mechanic, a love that would never leave him, drawing him more and more to the world he now lives in; as he moved into the world of teaching mechanical studies, he put right the poor education by completing as many qualifications as he could.

As children came along, responsibility beckoned, life was happy and quaint, but the desire for adrenaline always bubbled. Now with all 3 children having jobs and lives of their own, Mark and his wife are living a fast paced adrenaline filled life and a desire to escape the "norms" of society.

Roaming Revelator is Mark's first book of a trilogy, a story inspired by real life stories and events that have only happened in the depth of imagination.

BV - #0034 - 130623 - C0 - 216/140/16 - PB - 9781912419852 - Matt Lamination